The Convoy

The Legend of the Future

Volume II

I0561661

The Convoy

The Legend of the Future
Volume II

by Luiza Dobrzyńska

TABLE OF CONTENTS

THE CONVOY
THE LEGEND OF THE FUTURE
BY LUIZA DOBRZYŃSKA

ORIGINALLY PUBLISHED IN POLAND ENTITLED KAWALKADA
IN 2013 BY EVANART.
***

TRANSLATED AND PUBLISHED IN ENGLISH WITH PERMISSION.
***

PAPERBACK ISBN: 978-1-7348606-8-9
EPUB ISBN: 978-1-3933192-3-8
***

WRITTEN BY LUIZA DOBRZYNSKA
PUBLISHED BY ROYAL HAWAIIAN PRESS
COVER ART BY TYRONE ROSHANTHA
TRANSLATED BY AGATA SUCHOCKA
PUBLISHING ASSISTANCE: DOROTA RESZKE
***

FOR MORE WORKS BY THIS AUTHOR, PLEASE VISIT:
WWW.ROYALHAWAIIANPRESS.COM
***

VERSION NUMBER 1.00

PROLOGUE

A couple of months ago Estrella Solis had been a teacher in a primary school in one of the South-American metropolises and her life had been an even flow. The world she had been living in was clean and ordered, the rules making the individual work for the common good. Criminals and handicapped who couldn't be fixed by bionic medicine, were eliminated. The laws of those days convicted Etta for solitude. Due to her defected genome, she was banned from breeding, and therefore men were not interested in marrying her. Women like her were often abandoned even by their own families. Craving some companionship, Etta had bought an AC – Android Companion – and was astonished how human-like the machine turned out to be. She thought her life to be stable and devoid of surprises, but one day her friend from the past days came with a proposition. Etta and her companion were to join a crusade for colonizing one of Jupiter's moons. Etta accepted the deal, not knowing the complexity of the government's plan and an amount of information that were hidden from the crusaders. Even before they had started a lot of unpredictable and not always pleasant things happened. It turned out that her seemingly honest friend hid a lot from Etta, and her brother-in-law was in reality a perverted murderer. And it was only the top of the mountain of trouble…

I

The Human Resources Center was busy and anxiety filled the air. They were all waiting for that one precious news, day by day, hour after hour, but the silence prevailed and nobody tried to explain it. The pioneers had no questions, but they were not aware that something was fishy, but the staff thrived in the constant nervousness, all of them: the administration, the scientists, even the cleaners. Only captain Willner seemed to remain calm.

"Launching such a crusade is a big deal," he was explaining while eating late supper with Etta and Veronica in the café. "Every last little screw must be tight in place, otherwise something really unfortunate might happen."

"Why are the officials on top silent?" asked Etta. "They hadn't answered not even one of our questions!"

Kirk shrug his shoulders and smoothed his prematurely gray hair. He was the one who had to release the tension and calm everybody down. As usual. But that was his job as the chief of the expedition and he was just performing it. And well.

"They have their reasons, little one. And we are here to wait and to obey, for the common good. Happiness of the one is not important, the most important is the common wellness. Aren't we being taught that simple truth from the cradle?"

He ceased to use the official title and from some time he was calling Etta "little one". One might assume he harbored some feeling for her, like a father, or maybe like a brother. Well, he cared for all of the crew, showering them with warmth and playing mister Nice, but Etta was his favorite for the reasons even he himself couldn't guess.

"The society is made of individuals!" Veronica barked buoyantly.

"Of course it is, Miss Hornet. But the times when the individual happiness was placed above the common good were the times of crime and social instability and riots. Etta is a historian, she could explain that to you. We have our own ways that led to create the social model that really works."

He was right. No matter what one thought about that, the rigid and strict criminal codex made people live in a cocoon of safety; the causes of drastic social life status differences completely erased.

It was easy to live, because everyone knew what was wanted of him or her. Was it even possible that people who were pampered and nurtured by their environment would work in the unknown, where life might turn into rough and hostile battlefield, like it was in times of American pioneers?

"I am afraid of migrating…" Etta whispered.

Kirk just smiled at her in that heart-warming way of his.

"We are all anxious, it's only natural. But don't you worry, my girls, I am sure the matters will be cleared in a couple of days!"

"Kirk, tell me one thing, do soldiers want to migrate?" Veronica asked, playing with her teaspoon absentmindedly.

The captain's eyes darkened a little and run aside.

"I will tell you that: many of them have their personal reasons. One of the soldiers is guilty of the death of his brother and the guilt haunts him wherever he goes. The kids were just playing and he had pushed his brother underwater in the bathtub, it was all just a game. The boy choked on water and died before the paramedics arrived. The parents have never forgiven, and wherever the man went, he was blemished with his deed. Only the army accepted him. I have no reasons to remain on Earth. And others have different their own motives, all of them equally important. None of them is forced to go."

Veronica just pushed a bit of her yellowish, almond cream into her mouth.

"I thought about killing my brother more than once. And no pangs of consciousness would eat me for sure," she murmured after swallowing.

"So it is good for you to go. It's better than committing a crime." The captain was not shocked by her statement.

Veronica had told him more than once how much she hated her younger brother. And it was not her own conviction, but the fault of her parents, but a fact was a fact.

"Why is it so that it is easier to come to terms with androids than with one's own family?" Etta's voice was barely audible.

"It is because they do not think as people think. They do not have our vile instincts, our human irrationality." Kirk stretched up. "All right, girls, I don't know your plans for the evening, but

I'm off for a shower and a good night's sleep. It's almost midnight and I am to be on the playground."

Veronica also thought the idea of getting some rest tempting.

Etta nevertheless wasn't sleepy at all. She felt unwell. The launching was approaching, and she felt like visiting her parents once more before she would soar to the stars. They were not all good and kind to her, but they were still her parents, and once she flies into the unknown, there would be no returning. Nobody could get out of the center, but she was pleasantly surprised that she could be granted the pass as a crew member.

"You can be gone no longer than twenty-four hours," The operating chief colonel Kovacs informed her. "The pass is a proof of the government's and generals' trust. No food and no drinks allowed."

"What do you mean?"

"I mean that you cannot eat anything from the unknown source. Collect some ratios in the base. And take this." He handed her a beautiful necklace – silver flower with a blue pearl in the center.

"Just press the pearl if anything unexpected happens. It is an emergency call," he explained. "Some problems occurred… lately."

Etta felt alarmed, but didn't intend to show that. She didn't want the chief to withdraw the pass after noticing she was afraid.

She put some elegant, civilian clothes on, made her hair up instead of pulling it back into a pony-tail and rushed to a landing spot where a small plane has already been awaiting her.

Etta didn't expect her parents to be happy with her visit, but so they were. Even her little twin brothers: Diogo and Nando, beamed at her as if forgetting that a "zero" sister was rather something to be ashamed of. Luckily enough, Nayeli was still at the medical center and Johnny had moved out long ago to live in Newark with his wife. Those two had forced Etta to move out and not to bother the family with her zero classification.

"We all thought you wouldn't bother yourself with visiting us anymore," Livia said with reproach, putting some cookies and tea on the table. "What about that colony at the other side of the world you were supposed to live at?"

The other side of the world…

Etta wanted so badly to tell her family where in reality she was supposed to be send to, but it was top secret. Nobody was to know.

"It is all scheduled," she murmured, "I cannot step back now, even if I wanted to. I am enlisted to the basic crew, I have even passed an exam to become an officer. I am bound to do what I have to do."

"Are you sure that you know what you're doing?" The tinge of care resounded in her father's voice. "They said that the other hemisphere is not ready to live there yet."

"Re-cultivation is a success. There is a spot there when the pioneers can settle. You know, dad, population is bound to grow, there will be a great demand for new settlements soon. There are many children among the pioneers, somebody must teach them. I am needed there."

"But why there? Is it so bad here?"

"No, mum! It's not that! A long, long time ago people arrived here from the place called Europe, from the other side of the world. I want to see that place as one of the first, after such a long time nobody hasn't been there." Etta couldn't make her mind to sip her tea.

Kovacs' warnings were ringing in her head, and even though it was absurd that her parents could be some terrorists, something has constantly whispered in her mind to stay point. She focused on keeping her face blank, she was never a good liar.

"I've seen some pictures once," her father said, rubbing at his chin, "It is hard to believe that people used to live in such a place. And that they intend to live there again."

"They must have been from the times before re-cultivation."

Umberto Solis just shook his head, not convinced at all. His face still kept its youngish looks, even though he has just turned fifty, and was now grave serious.

"You are hiding something, girl. I am a biochemist, don't you forget that. I know too much of nature to believe that the soil once contaminated as such could be miraculously healed. I don't know what stinks so much in that case, but I still don't like it."

Etta knew all too well that her father was right. The remnants of European and Africans came here to stay, knowing that their native grounds would be useless for generations. Some remote parts of Asia harbored some people still, but Europe turned into a different, hostile planet. And it was all because of bombings with nuclear rockets, in some minor wars that lasted just few weeks, on two different continents. The pollution, radiation and the power of bombs shattered everything. Refugees made to America,

Australia and New Zealand, keeping with themselves so a lot of small, closed settlements with strange speech and strange, archaic customs sprouted. Little Ireland (doctor's O'Leary's family came from there), Little Sweden, Little Poland – all of those names became recognizable. They even formed some armed troops that were named after the lost world: African, European, and Eurasian, Balkan, it was all done to commemorate the fatherlands lost forever. In the beginning the refugees didn't even unpack their bags, hoping for going home, but it was soon obvious that their homelands would remain polluted for centuries. So they had to settle on the new grounds, among Americans, Australians and Islanders, who were often not happy with the new neighbors. It took some time for people to come to terms with one another.

"Dario was also saying something was fishy," the mother said, "He was to check what it was and for sure he discovered something, and therefore he was imprisoned. And he is to be executed! Why, I ask you? Your sister will not manage without him! Etta, you know something, tell me! What is really going on?"

Etta was silent, still clutching to the cup she was holding in her hands. She sipped some purple drink and suddenly, to the surprise of her parents, and even to her own, she burst with tears. The cup rolled on the carper and the girl hid her face in the hands, trying to muffle the sobs that were chocking her. She had never felt so bad before. No wonder they were implanting some chips into their tongues. No wonder she was trained to recognize all of the poisons and chemical inductors known to humankind, and that was what she was tasting now, the probe number 54. Her parents, the parents she loved so much…!

"What's wrong, sis?" Diogo's words were not penetrating, as if her ears were clutched with cotton.

The boy was surprised, he didn't know, for sure, but the faces of her parents bore a bitter look of disappointment.

"Why?!" Etta shouted accusingly, stopping her tears. "You've never loved me, but why do you treat me as your enemy? What have I done to you?"

The Solis exchanged glances, as if saying to each other: 'So she noticed!"

"Calm down," the father said roughly. "You are the one who treat us like enemies. You are the one who hides everything. We only wanted to know why was Dario arrested."

"Nayeli got sick after it happened," The mother nodded, "Itati and Amador are going to grow up without a father. We just want to know, why? Dario is such a good boy-"

"Dario is a murderer!" Etta screamed. "He killed a man! Nayeli must have known his plans, I bet she would have been arrested if the illness hadn't got her! And if you are both so after them that you try to suck the information out of me using some chemicals, means only that you already know too much!"

"We don't-"

"So how come you got the possession of this filth?!"

"They have found it in Dario's room," Nando stepped in. "He owns huge amount of that stuff. Don't treat us like we were fools, mum, he didn't intend to use those for some legal business."

"How dare you...?"

"You think he is some hero, but he is just a rascal, "Diogo backed his brother. "He made Nayeli yield to him like some slave, she ceased to think on her own. It is good that the kids won't have such a father. We will do better at bringing them up."

They both looked mad.

"Enough!" Umberto rose from his chair. "You know nothing of Dario! Why aren't you interested in Estrella having so many secrets, not trusting her family?"

Etta also stood up. She was not crying anymore. She was furious.

"If you cannot get the simple fact that I work for the government now and I need to keep my matters confidential, so be it." She said. "I just wanted to say my farewell to you. I didn't expect to be seen as some hostile agent from a spy novel!"

"That's unfair!"

Etta was gliding in a public transportation slider. It was unfair that she had to choose between her family and her orders. They were still her family, nothing changed in that matter, even though they treated her as a stranger. She leaned her forehead against the window, thinking about visiting the school she used to teach at, but coping with the kids' questions would be too much. She decided to go to the King Park instead. The slider stooped at Bolivar Street. She headed towards the gate. She loved the place, she could walk freely for hours, not getting anyone's attention. The city architects outdid themselves by designing the place to make it look as natural as possible: one could swear that the grass and flowers were real, that the tree leaves really rustled, like in the natural reserve park. Even the pond and swans floating on the water looked real, one could almost touch them. Etta thought about the first day at Human Resources Center when she saw little Timmy dive into the pond. The boy saw real water for the first time and couldn't know it was dangerous. She also had no idea that the park there wasn't just a hologram illusion and some synthetic designs, but real trees, flowers and water. Surprisingly, she preferred the artificial one now. King Park was clean, sterile, she felt safe here. The real nature she came to know was disturbing and filthy. She was used to live in the clean city environment and just felt bad dealing with nature. Doctor O'Leary used to laugh at her when she withdrew from it. She didn't know why, but that strange man had always seemed weird to her.

Etta walked through the alleys, then sat at the fountain that wasn't really a fountain and closed her eyes. The thought about the flight seemed absurd to her, for the very first time. She belonged to this clean and ordered world, why would she want to abandon it and head for some unknown planet? She almost dozed in her doubts and jumpstarted, when somebody grabbed her arms.

The twins were here. Their chests heaving, hair tousled.

"It's just us, don't worry!" Diogo exclaimed. "We want you to know that we don't share the parents' rights! We've never liked Dario. He was such a slim shady! He didn't fool us!"

"But what's more important," Nando broke in, looking around, "you are being followed!"

"Who?"

"We don't know exactly, some Dario's mates. They used to come around and talk to dad a lot, we were being sent to daycare when it happened. We overheard them saying that they observe everything."

"And dad called them right after you left!" Diogo added. "He thinks it would be better that they locked you somewhere, so you couldn't come back to wherever you are living now." He was stuttering, still looking around, making Etta finally get up and start to look around herself.

"Thanks, boys!" she murmured. "I will be fine. But why are you here…?"

"Because we don't believe them all!"

She wanted so much to interrogate the brothers thoroughly, but they had no time for it. If the kids hadn't made all that up, she had to head for the base as soon as possible. She decided to walk across the park and take the slider number 5 that ended his route at the suburbs, ale the military landing. They should collect her from there. She kissed the flushed boys good bye.

"You are great, kiddos!" she whispered affectionately. The brothers hugged her back, so hard she felt a pang in her heart. She would Miss them greatly, but she couldn't tell them it was their last meeting.

She turned left and rushed up the alley, trying to keep her pace steady, she didn't want anybody to suspect anything. If the twins had followed her, the observer must have noticed them. Was that person aware that the boys wanted to talk to her? Was she really followed?

"Miss Solis, wait! I need to talk to you!"

She turned around and saw Welles, the teacher who took her class after she resigned. He was walking, all smiles, in his immaculate white suit. He must have finished his work and decided to rest a little in this peaceful place. Etta smiled back at him and waved. She had no time to get to know the man, but he had a reputation of being engaged in what he did and having good understanding of kids. She stopped, grabbed by an urgent need of getting to know how the little minions were doing: Jodie, Waylon, and Tracy, all of those little people she was separated from forever.

Welles was quite close when two dark shapes jumped out of the shrubs, screaming, and grabbed his legs. Etta was watching helplessly at the man struggling with her little brothers.

"Run Etta!" Diogo screamed.

"Run for your life!" Nando was even louder, he was clutching to the suit with his both hands. "He is the one who talked to dad!!"

Even before she grasped the meaning of the situation she was running to the closest exit. She pushed the pearl in the necklace hard, hearing some click sound, she really hoped it ran some kind of alarm and wasn't just a cheap trick. Welles couldn't set the trap alone, there must have been more of them here. She noticed that running was not as hard as it used to be before she had started the trainings at the camp. And she used to nag about them so much! Mima Radovič was merciless, she was dragging them along the park and running tracks, but it was effective. They had been working out together, bot soldiers and civilians, and they became tougher, even gained some immunity towards common sickness. Etta wasn't even breathing heavily when she finally got to the gate.

They were waiting in the street. Who men wearing youth fashion: dark clothes, legs broad at the bottom and sewn with mock-leather patches. She managed to notice that when one of them stepped behind her, and the other tried to press some cloth to her face, a sedative to be sure. She kicked hard at his knee, just like her martial arts sensei, Omi Mi-Kori had taught her, and tried to release her arms grabbed from behind, screaming like crazy. The assailant gagged her and she didn't manage to set herself free, but the policeman riding nearby was alarmed by the struggle.

"What is going on here?" he shouted, putting his motorcycle to a halt.

The one Etta had kicked produced some tool out of nowhere and brushed the policeman's arm with it, the device sputtering sparks and burning the hole in the man's sleeve. He hid behind his bike, reaching for the gun. Another two men appeared, all clad the same, and Welles was running towards them, still chased by the boys. Etta bit hard on the man's hand and used his surprise to jump over the motorcycle to crouch by the officer, instead of running blindly away.

"Careful, my brothers are there!" she howled, thinking at the same time about some new kind of weapon the rouge used. An ordinary gun wouldn't burn through the bernit uniform. It was tougher than kevlar.

"Relax, I'm not shooting kids!" he hissed. "What is this mess?"

Etta didn't know how to answer, but she was saved by the hoard of soldiers who filled the street. Two of them dragged Etta into a tank plane, the rest hurled to arrest the assailants. She noticed the policeman assisting them before the blinds in the windows rolled down and the vehicle shot upwards, to the basis.

She was safe.

"We managed to break the international anti-government organization, The Green October, all thanks to you." Colonel Kovacs told her. "They are extremely dangerous people. Please accept my gratitude!"

Etta was silent. The realization that she had been used as bait wasn't pleasant. She got the notion that there was no other way to do it, but she still felt bad, and was even filled with dread of her parents. If they related to those people, for sure they would also be arrested. The colonel was looking at her from under frown eyebrows, playing with the necklace she had given back.

"There is a problem with your brothers, though," he said finally. "We cannot send them back home, they know too much."

"So...?"

"So, they will join the colonists."

"My parents would never approve of that!"

"They still have Itati and Amador to take care of. I have no idea how it had come to be that the grandchildren were put in their custody... The recommendation of Colonel Gongadze was otherwise. And still they have the kids, apparently thanks to his letter."

"Perhaps he had really recommended them as foster parents?"

"No, he hadn't. I know every word of that letter. If we were not in such a rush, we would inquire into the matter. The young ones remind with your parents. We should put some charges against them, though. But we won't. There are no clear evidence blaming them for being in the underground, they were obviously unaware of Dario Cantoralles schemes. We can release them, I think."

"Thank you," Etta whispered. She was sad, but relieved at the same time.

"You're welcome. You may go."

On the way to her room Etta was thinking about the whole matter. Somebody had obviously changed the body of the letter which Gongadze had sent to court. But who had skills and chance to do such a thing? There was just one answer: Raul. She would have to talk to him about that, but not tonight. Tonight, she was dead tired.

II

Etta and Veronica were sitting at the half-melted ice-cream.

Etta was gloomy and down, her friend looked no better.

"Well, it all turned out quite harmless," she said, trying to sound cheerfully.

"Still, I feel pretty bad about the matter. Think what my parents go through now!"

"If they had stayed off those matters, nothing so epic would have happened!" Veronica was calm, she just spooned her ice-cream. "And those brothers of your, they had more brains than your parents!"

"And what is the outcome of it?" Etta sneered. "They are being treated like refugees from the past ages! Like some minor criminals from the Middle Ages, or those from the times of eco-Armageddon! The law didn't take into consideration the age of people then, everyone was punished alike. The judge could make a six-year-old work in the labor camp, just for stealing a lump of sugar of some fruit. One orange or an apple could make a kid drop dead from the drudge."

"You are exaggerating. Your brothers are not being mistreated, and this is not a prison. I bet they see it as a great adventure. And there is nothing you can do about the situation."

"I cannot even pay them a visit now…"

"You'll survive it. It so cool you have such devoted brothers. Mine wouldn't help me even if I were to be decapitated. Damned bastard! He told me once when I were sick that he wished I died," Veronica spit out.

Her parents got permission for only two pregnancies, so her seven-year younger brother, Burton, was the pupil of their eye, the spoilt prince allowed to run loose. What was worse, he was categorized "3" and not "0" like his older sister.

"Don't you get so bitter, my dear. You don't have to care what they all think anymore," Etta smiled at her warmly. "You are independent, you have high position and important role here, and a lot of nice people to work with. You achieved much more than your little brother ever would."

"It's good they are all far away." Veronica waved at the waiter to order some more ice-cream. They were the remedy for all worries and she could devour an amount of an ice-berg of those.

On the way back from the café the friends decided to go to scientific labs. They were curious about Raina's progress. That unexpected companion of Leonard Derkacz became their close friend, which was surprising if one considered how much harm had been done to her in the past. Whether they wanted it or not, the girls got acquainted with Leonard, and once they got used to his appearance, he didn't seem so ugly to them. His strange-looking face was somewhat interesting, even his bony figure gained some charm. Once you came to know him, Derkacz turned out to be quite nice. He was unable by design to be selfish, deceitful or mean, but he was also a bit too serious. He seemed to have no sense of humor at all, but his other features made everyone like him nevertheless. As a superb cyber scientist and a master at andro-psyche, he could draw Raina out of her stupor, so she ceased to behave like autistic child. She has been learning fast, as all androids, but she harbored the delicacy and shyness which attracted all to her. She followed all the orders immediately and fast, as if being afraid of punishment. She also followed Leonard as if she were his pet dog, and always looked confused when he wasn't around. She was unusual, that was more than obvious, and even McLean O'Leary admitted that he hadn't seen a model like her before.

"But it doesn't prove anything," he said, "There are not so many androids, and she is just the first one somebody had tortured. She was bombed with invalid input and misinformed while her psyche was forming, and all those shaped her personality to make it just as we see it now. It is sad, actually, but we cannot turn any of it back."

The girls didn't manage to the scientific labs. Suddenly the sharp, piercing sound ringed, meaning: "All hands to the control center, immediately!" And 'immediately' meant exactly that in the case, one couldn't hold back. The call was meant for everyone, from captains to the lowliest cleaners, and so far, hadn't been emitted even once. Something unexpected must have happened.

Etta and Veronica rushed to the control center, almost running. The auditorium of the check-in room was half-full when they got there. Captain Willner arrived right after them, combing nervously his wet hair, as if he had jumped out of the shower. The last one to arrive was Doctor O'Leary, in his pajama shirt unbuttoned. Once woken up by his assistant he just didn't care to change. If it was so urgent, people didn't pay attention to the clothes on the back of one of the departments' chiefs. When all the people assigned to the crew were gathered, electronic devices closed the doors and the holographic projection of the Admiral of the global forces Kondratiuk shown at the speaking pulpit.

"Welcome, ladies and Gentlemen," it uttered the greetings. "It's no time to be sorry for dragging you out of beds, it is enough to say that your time has come. The colonists will proceed now to the medical center, where they will be aestheticized and put to sleep, and then transported to the capsules. As you all know, they will travel sedated and in the state of hibernation, it will be safer. All of the crew and the guards will proceed to your rooms now to collect the items allowed on board. You will then proceed as enlisted to the vehicles which would take you to the ferry launching area. You will be taken to the crafts waiting for you at the orbit. When the convoy launches, the details about the route will be delivered to you automatically. The Earth wishes you safe trip and farewell."

"Any of that sounds familiar?" Etta asked.

"None. Full conspiracy, as we now know." Veronica murmured. "Go grab your stuff, we will meet at the park lot."

The luggage with the essentials packed, one bag per person, was waiting ready for many days. Raul, asking no questions, locked the room and followed his mistress to the check-in, where the vehicles crouched waiting. They looked like ordinary cargo carriers, but inside they were more like civil jets. Troops of soldiers were trafficking people to the machines, in the remote part of the launching spot the hibernating capsules were gathered. The colonists were to be unconscious throughout the trip, oblivious to everything around them. Etta was sorry for a brief moment that she wouldn't be one of those. She was to be locked in the space craft for four months, and she haven't even seen the plans or pictures of it. The only thing she knew about it was that it was huge, it had been constructed in space, not on the ground. If it was done on the face of the planet, the launching would destroy such vast grounds that it wouldn't be possible to keep the matter confidential. That was what Willner said once.

Etta sat in her seat, Raul next to her. Two rows ahead the captain was seated, Veronica and Rasmus next to him. Doctor O'Leary, his assistant and Raina sat nearby. Their presence should put Etta at ease, it meant they would be travelling on one craft, but she felt anxious somewhat. The realization that she couldn't step back now was overwhelmingly dreadful.

III

The short flight and docking in the belly of the huge craft was so ordinary, as if they had travelled from one city to another. Although Etta didn't like flying, there was nothing frightening or mysterious in those. She felt like that now, as if she were about to step out in some friendly city like New Palermo or Singapore but the illusion was shattered once she stepped out of the vehicle.

It was a windowless hangar of some sorts, where three small, empty crafts were clasped to the walls, waiting for the passengers. The seals of Earth Union and the 'Viking 01' symbols were painted on the sides of the ships. The young man wearing black, tight-fit suit with the pilot's badge on the chest and a tiny tattoo at the side of his forehead, meaning he was a 100 percent mentally stable unit, was waiting for them.

"My name is Camus de Bernal, I am the chief pilot," he introduced himself, saluting to captain Willner. "Welcome aboard Viking 01, captain, and all of the crew. Follow me to the quarters."

He turned around and touched a slant panel in the wall. The inner hangar door slid open, it led to the lower corridor foamed in plastic. It remained Etta of some scientific institute building, all gray and neutral. There were doors paneling the walls, the holographic images of the natural Earth habitats separating them. There were labs and storage rooms hidden behind them. The private quarters were hidden deeper inside. The cabins were big enough to cradle bunk bed in each, some in-built lockers or cupboards, a table that could been slid out of the wall and three chairs. There was a mirror on one wall and a small washbasin with antibacterial aerosol diffuser over it. The tubes in which one could clean the whole body were also waterless. It was too precious in space to waste it for washing. Chemicals and compressed air were to keep Etta clean for four months. The claustrophobic space was tamed by a screen in front of the beds, on which one could project anything, from the craft database or personal device. Those who owned the Companions, were to live with them, the singles were to decide with whom they would want to stay. All of them wanted to sniff through the living section once they were suited. Only the paramedics rushed to the capsules to check if the colonists were safe and properly secured for the trip. The cargo crew went to check the supplies. The technology that would enable to break inorganic substance into atoms and clustering them back into soy-like, digestible pulp had already existed, but it took time and energy to produce that kind of food. It was an alternative nobody was eager to use. The engineers and guards were scattered to check the technical conditions of the craft and extinguish any signs of sabotage. They were particularly interested in the main captain's deck: the round room filled with steering consoles and panoramic screens. They didn't manage to get into cockpit, separated from the rest of the room with clear panels. Only the pilots and the captain were allowed in there.

The craft could also be controlled from the captain's deck. It was a security procedure if some pilot decided to turn into Kamikaze mode. The pilots were only humans, even though trained from the young years, their psychic profiles stable, but every possibility in the case of human beings had to be secured.

"Why hadn't they trained droids for pilots?" Etta inquired.

Kirk Willner smiled heartwarmingly.

"There are some tasks, my dear, which can only be performed by humans. Don't worry, the commanders had designed it right!"

One of the pilots rose and stepped out of the cockpit.

"Colonel Joao Jimenez reporting, Captain. Ready for launching!" he barked, saluting with an outstretched hand.

"At ease, colonel!" Willner sat in the commander's seat and turned the inner communicator. "Attention, all the crew! This is your captain calling! All hands on deck, I repeat, all hands at the main deck!"

The training was successful: in just a few minutes all who weren't hibernated, human, bot and droids, appeared at the captain's deck. And those were not many at all: six security officers, cyber scientists O'Leary and Derkacz, three engineers (the other two remained in the engine room, and Aisha Bahrani was to be re-located to the Viking 03 as their main technician), seven general technicians, diet specialist, Etta and Veronica. And the three droids: Raul, Brent and Raina. The latecomers were two nurses, two medical assistants and the medical equipment technician with doctor Xiao. The chief doctor was relocated to Viking 02, where Oksana Wysocka and little Timmy were sleeping, He wanted to be at their side.

The small place of the deck seemed crowded all of a sudden.

"Attention, the cockpit!" the captain said to the microphone. "Release the clutches!"

"Release the clutches, done!" the answer came.

"The clutches released!" the pilot melded.

"Launch the manual steering!"

"Launch the manual steering, done! Manual steering launched!"

"Hold!" Willner switched the communicator to the remaining crafts. "Viking 02, Viking 03, Viking 04, Viking 05, preparing for launching!"

The answers were like mantra: "Viking 02, ready for launching!". "Viking 03, ready for launching!", "Viking 04, ready for launching!", "Viking 05, ready for launching!"

"Launching every five minutes!" Kirk switched the communicator back, "Full power!"

"Full power, sir!"

The launching was a lot less thrilling Etta had expected. The floor under her feet shuddered, the pictures behind the windows switched and... froze.

"Are we flying?" she asked, full of doubt, looking at Raul.

"We are," he confirmed.

"We can't I see the motion?"

"Amateur..." Doctor O'Leary sneered. "The stars are too far away, kid. Their position won't change, they won't melt into the smears of light, like in some movie, even if we gain the maximum speed.

The picture of Admiral Kondratiuk blinked at the main screen.

"Greetings, ladies and gentlemen. You have successfully started for this pioneer trip. Today is the first day of your brand-new life, the life that is not dependent on Earth anymore. You have become its ambassadors. Now, after you cannot turn back, I can tell you the real goal of your trip. You are not heading to Enceladus. That tiny moon was never our goal, it is too small to even have an atmosphere, and it is made entirely of ice. The experimental station at its surface is a small self-sustaining ecosphere, which can harbor just a few people. Your goal is father away, beyond the Kuiper's belt. Have you ever heard of Nemesis?"

"The hypothetical dark star…" Veronica started, but got silent immediately. She was stunned, like everyone else. Only O'Leary was calm and bitter, as if something bad has just happened, something that he had actually expected.

Kondratiuk nodded.

"Nemesis was once nick-named "the dark star", he said, "and it is quite an appropriate name. Of course, something like that doesn't exist, but our attempts to find it brought some quite unexpected discovery: the micro-star, and it seemingly works according to laws unknown to us. The most probable origin of it is splitting some matter off our sun. Its particles floated through the solar system and wound around the dying brown midget, the one that was probably the ancestor of our sun in this part of the universe. And that is how Jewel had come to being: the tine star, warm enough for the planet encircling it to develop some forms of life. As we assume its solar system consists of the items that got magnetized by it, but those are the matters of no consideration to you. The whole situation took place in the times of the forming of our planet, due to the same cataclysm that caused moon splitting from Earth, and the planets were just pulled towards the stars some billion years later. Jewel is placed in such altitude from the sun that it was impossible for the scientists from the past ages to confirm its existence, even though they had assumed it might be there. The huge dust discus blocks all signals, and only after the station Michio1 started to collect the data, being placed sideways towards it, Jewel's existence could be confirmed."

The animated graph of the small system appeared on the screen.

"As you can see, it is impossible to spot those from Earth. When the astronomers got the detailed data of the star, they also got the information of the planets circling around them. There is a twin planet of Earth there. And the intensity of the light of Jewel and the spectrum of it won't change during next twenty-five ages or so. It is more than enough for us. The discovery started the research that lasted almost a hundred years. The analyses we had run allowed us to send robots and machines there to build the basis for the future colony. We hadn't known if we would be able to use any of it, the government resisted for a long time, but finally the project was accepted and now you are where you are."

"Nobody has warned us that we would be send so far!" Aisha Bahrani shouted. "It means that the communication with Earth will be broken at one point or another!" Her voice was getting hysterical.

They could hear similar protests from the remaining vehicles, as the communication was switched into forum mode. The captains were appealing for order, the doctor was called somewhere to give some sedative to someone. Etta eyed Willner, who just has got slightly pale, but shown no other signs of anxiety. He produced an inhalator from his pocket and made sobbing Aisha to breath in a dose. Then he took the mike in his hand and shouted:

"Order, Order, all decks! Let's listen to the Admiral! And don't we all forget that we are the selected units of the high social use and stable mentality, and not a heard of scared monkeys!"

His words made an adequate impression, the voices were hushed, people calmed down, and Kondratiuk could continue his speech.

"Thank you, captain. We had our reasons to keep the whole matter confidential. And your hysterical reaction proves we were right. Although you are the fruit of the loom, you could not be able to stand the tension at the realization of the importance of your Mission and its goal. You cannot look back now, just keep looking forward! You are heading towards the planed named Patris. The dwellings and supplies are waiting for your arrival. The database of all possible human resources will help you to establish some environmental-friendly industry there, which would prevent the colony to draw back. The Earth will know that you would be waiting there, ready for welcoming new migrants from the Earth. And a time of a mass-migration may be at hand. Consider yourself lucky, you will not see the cataclysms and catastrophes which would force us to abandon our planet. Well, those of us who will survive. We would never be able to build enough number of space crafts to save everyone. And when the time comes, people will kill for a place in the craft. And I hope I won't live long enough to see it."

"Is it so bad?" Leonid Derkacz asked. Both he and his boss didn't look quite scared by the situation. His square face beamed with scientist's anticipation.

"Will be, soon." The Admiral replied. "The information about the asteroid approaching our planet are confirmed. It is not one object, but a herd of them, the trajectory of each crossing with the orbit of the Earth. We might disturb the trajectories, we might not. If any of those objects hit the planet, it would cause the series of tsunamis and the emission of gas and ash that would cause the global warming first, and then post-nuclear-like winter. The atmosphere would be polluted, the soil and water radiated. The life will be wiped out of our planet for a very long time. "

The silence fell after the last statement. Each of them thought of somebody who was left behind and realized, that there were worst things that being send in a comfortable space craft to the unknown planet. Nobody felt like protesting and shouting anymore. Kondratiuk broke his effective brought his speech to a close:

"We support you with all of our hearts. Be strong, save the heritage of humankind and remember, that the wisdom drawn from the mistakes of your ancestors is there for you to use. The Earth greets you and wishes you good luck!"

Etta looked around. People still looked surprised, but weren't scared anymore. She was calm, nevertheless. After a while she felt somebody holding her hand. It was Raul.

Etta scooped her ratio of the nutrient paste and sat at the table. The diet technician was just experimenting with the hydrolyzed concentrates that were produced on Earth. He managed to produce something that – with the huge amount of good will – could be compared to a baby soup of meat and vegetables, with a note of mushroom. Etta knew better that it was the taste of some artificial species of saprophytes, rich in vitamins and microelements.

"I will Miss the crisps and peanuts the most... and pretzels!" she said to Raul, who seated himself next to her. He didn't need to eat, he was there just to keep her company.

"Five meals a day, not bad!" the droid remained her. "The doctors were uncompromised in that matter. They claimed that portioning the daily ratio into three bigger and two small parts will work better than traditional three gluttonous meals. But I cannot see the point of imbibing the micro-portions for brunch and in tea time... Well, we wouldn't get tea and biscuits for sure!" Etta sneered.

You could as well swallow some nutrients pills instead. It would save time, space and the cook's work."

"It wouldn't be good for our health. And our psyche for sure. Our bowels need to digest, they cannot remain empty and motionless. It could cause much trouble in the whole system."

The android was silent for a while.

"I lack some information in those matters..." Raul seemed confused and Etta smiled. It wasn't a common reaction in a droid.

"You cannot know it all. Well, you could, since your storage and memory are vast, but you won't achieve that without learning."

"I can learn."

Veronica approached their table. She looked spotless and elegant, as usual, even with bernite uniform on and head shaved. Keeping clean in space was essential and hard at the same time, so getting rid of hair was a matter of no discussion. The women understood, but did it with broken hearts. They all got used to their new looks all too soon, and it wasn't that bad as they all had assumed. And Veronica looked good in any situation. She could be mistaken for a fashion magazine model, even if she were clad in a garbage sack and sprinkled with sooth.

"How are you, Etta?" she asked, sitting. "I had to sedate two hysterics today, I hope you will not give me more work to do! Doctor Xiao was sure it would happen, we must be ready in case anything went wrong. Or everything. Even though the crafts seem huge, some of the crew will become claustrophobic for sure."

"That's going to be a party…"

"It is. We are to check in at the captain's in an hour, remember?"

"Of course I do. And those will be aplenty before we get to Patris."

Veronica put a spoonful of food into her mouth absentmindedly, thinking about something remote. She swallowed and asked her friend:

"You really think we will ever get there? And if we do, whatever the hell awaits us there?"

Etta felt sorry for her. She was the chief coordinator of the civilian crew, and therefore she couldn't show any weakness. Doctor O'Leary laughed that if captain Willner was the father of the expedition, she was definitely the mother of it. And she was so frighteningly young, and unexpected at the space travel, as most of them were. They were the ones who started to write that chapter in the humankind history, the pioneers of the unknown terra. The space stations on Venus and Mars were functioning the Moon-mining was a branch of industry, and even though longer space travels were possible in theory, nobody had considered practicing them so far. There was a lot of talking about adapting Europe: the moon of Jupiter, about terra-forming of Titan, but apart from talking nothing happened in those matters. And now they were sending people beyond the solar system...

"We do not know what awaits us there, really," she said, grave serious. "I checked the analysis. There is oxygen, water, and plants. And nothing more is confirmed. It's a lot, but it is nothing at the same time. But now we must focus on organizing the life here. We will worry later for what comes later. If it comes at all."

"True. We will be locked on those flying coffins for two years or so, it's time to get used to the idea."

"We'll manage."

"Sure, cause there are no other options."

Veronica sounded cheerful, but she couldn't really imagine organizing her life now. She could plan few months ahead, but years? It was beyond her comprehension.

"You have to realize that we are doomed if we won't manage to find and land on Patris," said the captain seriously. "The most powerful engines won't be able to push us to another location suitable for settling. Not in a span of an average human life. And adjusting Vikings to carry multigenerational crew and settlers is impossible. In space and the gravity that varies and fluctuates fetuses cannot develop properly. They would deform and malfunction. And even if the children were born, it wouldn't be possible to bring them up successfully in this claustrophobic space. They would suffer some serious mental distortions, I am quite sure of that. We cannot risk like that. The supplies wouldn't be sufficient. The crew members are all sterile, if we woke up the colonists, they would eat them out in no time. Patris is our only chance. Let's just hope we will get there."

"Does it really exist?" asked doctor Xiao, the petit, nervous Chinese woman. Her face was longish and elfish, and her eyebrows the perfect, thin arches. She was the daughter of a professor who was the chief of organization of the journey on the Earth. She was supposed to be damned intelligent, with the IQ over the magic number of 160.

"It does. I have checked all the data, using my captain access. It was really discovered a hundred years ago. Half a century ago the satellites and probing crafts were sent there, and the last two decades was sending the machines to build the settlements there. It is against the rule of keeping the space clean, but there was no other way. Where there's a will, there's a way, nothing truer in the humankind present situation. We had to modify the planet a little bit if we want to really live there. But a lot more is to be done, so be prepared for labor."

"Couldn't androids help?" Veronica asked.

"They could, but we would have to set the clear rules." Doctor O'Leary murmured. "And we would have to supervise them."

"What do you mean, doctor?" The captain encouraged his interlocutor.

"Working with the droids is not an easy task. They can misinterpret the orders, as they cannot develop the true intelligence. They cannot interpret human mimics, they only follow verbal communicates. If anyone shouts: "I'm falling!" the droid won't help the person, it would hear only the statement. We communicate in a way that is incomprehensible for them sometimes, using the code only people understand.

"Raul had saved little Timmy when he was drowning, even though he was not ordered to do so!" Etta exclaimed.

"Raul, Miss Solis, is atypical." the doctor pressed. "He makes his decisions while analyzing the data that he had remembered, the data that had been induced earlier, no longer available for the current use in different units. I haven't figured out yet what causes him to think in that pattern. But without human instinct he can as well decide to do something improper, even dangerous. And if he decides like that... I just claim, that the droids need control if they are to work with us. So, they wouldn't be effective anyway."

"Let's get back to Patris. "The biologist, Callum, broke in. "So Patris is real. Well, what is it like? What do we know about it?"

The captain looked at his tablet.

"The climate varies, similar like on the Earth. The flora is luscious, the water aplenty. The average atmosphere pressure is one hundred and one point three hundred twenty five milibars, and that is at the sea level, the equator is twenty-two degrees, the average temperature sixteen Celsius, and it doesn't change much. There are two more planets in Jewel solar system, but there are no data of it. There is life on Patris, the material collected at the planet's surface confirms that. Some people had been sent there before the Global Cosmic Program was cancelled. But it is gone and nobody knows what had happened to them. Only the standard procedural emergency call got back to the Earth."

"I've heard of that, The Hawking craft challenge," O'Leary murmured.

"And that is all we have. It is enough to survive, don't you think? But we must get there first, ladies and gentlemen. And if we manage to get there at all. And to do so, we must set some rules. So, I'm listening carefully to your reports. Doctor Xiao, what is the situation?"

The Chinese stirred, taken out of her thoughts.

"The main medical center is at Viking 02," she started. "Doctor Gongadze had organized the operating room and the intensive care unit. There is a medical point at each craft, enough to cure minor diseases of the crew."

"Technician section, report!"

"We have a vast supply of spare parts and the materials to improvise some alternatives, if we run out of spares. There is a crafts unit on Viking 04, in case we need to produce some parts. Everything works perfectly so far. The chief engineer ordered filling of the technical control sheets daily and bringing them directly to her." Woznansky said.

"What about the nutrition section?"

The technician, Stig Larson, of Norway descent, felt like getting up, then sat back again.

"We have a five-tear supply of lyophilizates. The hydroponic breed of algae and GM saprophytes will let us to save one quarter of the supply every year. The water is the problem, of course. The closed circuit will be infused with the byproducts of atomic synthesis. The technicians managed to launch the effective hydrogen atoms distillation system, we can find them out there."

"In vacuum?" Kovacs asked with disbelief.

"Space is not empty." Larson continued. "There are circa one hundred atoms in each square centimeter of so called vacuum. It seems not much, but we are moving at high speed, and the collectors are drawing the atoms in the radius of fifty meters from the surface of the shield."

"That type of hydrogen is highly instable." Sakura, to chemist, interfered.

"It doesn't matter, really. The tanks are sending the particles to the further proceedings, so the energy in them isn't too high. And we are successful at the procedure, there were two centimeters of water gathered in the tank number one this morning. And if we tried to drink it, we would have to supply the microelements as the water is completely pure. But that water is just of an emergency use, it will supply the closed circuit. And if anyone asked me, I wouldn't like to launch the machines for producing nutrients out of re-sequenced atoms. I don't trust the technologies which claim they could produce food out of sand."

"Databases?"

"All databanks available, computers working perfectly," reported Etta briefly.

"What about the crew's morale?"

"Well, that is difficult. I think it is going to be our main issue," Veronica said. "We must be ready to face some suicidal attempts, nervous breakdowns and aggression strikes."

"Well…" The captain looked at his notes again. "I need to tell you one more thing. Something you must know as the core of the crew. We were not sent for that Mission because we were the best. I know that Admiral Kondratiuk had underlined that. But it isn't the truth. Well, it is, sort of. We are the best selected from the worst."

The simmer ran through the gathering.

"The vision of the inevitable catastrophe made the government select those of us, who were not needed on the Earth. They couldn't have sent their aces, as they are needed down there, to try to save the planet. And I am not telling you that to make you down. On the contrary: the recognition of our flaws, the realization we are not super-humans, that will make us co-operate successfully. We cannot think of solo games, of epic heroic attempts. No lone riders on my crew. Do I make myself clear?"

The nods followed, only doctor O'Leary smiled bitterly, his skinny face twisted.

"I need to know one thing, captain as a chief coordinator," Veronica asked.

"Go on, Miss Hornet, ask."

"I know that it is not the pleasant issue, but we need to consider the situation of committing a crime. There is a prison on Viking 05, but what if that crime is murder, or attempt of murder? I don't need to remind you that the global Crime Code, paragraph sixty-six, states that the punishment for that is death. I'm not talking of euthanasia cases, but that issue is described in the medical ethics books."

"So, what is your question, exactly, Miss Hornet, if you know all the above?"

"Will you authorize performing the sentence? And who would do it? I won't let soldiers to become hangmen, even if you approved of it."

"Don't you worry about it now," said Willner coldly. "There is one simple solution to that."

"And that would be…?"

"I will perform the sentence."

Loud giggle of Doctor O'Leary broke the silence. He seemed to love the irony of the situation, and couldn't stop but comment on it:

"We are all so pathetically funny here!" He got up. "The heroes, the savers of humankind! The conquerors of stars! Don't make me laugh! We will shit our pants at the first signs of emergency or the outer danger!"

"We will clean ourselves then and send our uniforms to dry-cleaners." The captain replied calmly. "We are only humans, let's accept that. We are just the crew who must take care of the colonists' safe trip. They are the most important here. They are the ones who were trained and perfected to survive in the potentially hostile environment. We are to protect them and make the journey as safe as possible, so they don't have to worry about those trivial things."

"Cute." Somebody concluded.

Willner tapped the holographic screen in the center of the table on.

"Attentions, all the decks! Report your status!"

Three dimensional picture of all the check-in rooms appeared in the screen. The commanders of the crafts: Lavell, Kaori, Krasusky and Halama were looking straight into the cameras, other members of the crew seemed at a loss. It seemed they have just completed the check-ins, and the stormy ones.

"Viking 02, reporting order on deck." Cyra Lavell was the first one to speak. "No malfunctions, equipment and machines work stable."

"Viking 03, the same here," Yoko Kaori added.

"Viking 04, some leakage in the cooling system had been detected, but we have fixed it. Apart from that all in order," reported Sasha Krasusky.

The last one to report was Marjem Halama, and Viking 05 was also all right. Etta was thinking about the history of humankind, and about the women's rights in particular. Well, they were definitely the badge of progress here: female commanders were in majority. It was not surprising at all, if one considered the number of zero males and females. Women were the majority here as well. Nobody was surprised to see the vast number of women among technician, scientists, even soldiers selected for the Mission. Men were the minority here.

"We stay connected for the whole time I want you to report every three hours. We go to rest at ten p.m. deck time, wake up at five a.m. All personnel are to meet every day for an hour of workout and another hour in the games room. No isolating from the colleagues. Once a week we meet in the movie room to enjoy a séance together. The coordinators will schedule the charts for each shift. All insubordinate will be punished by cutting the food ratios of arrest, depending on the weight of the deed. Dismiss!"

The picture hovering above the table shimmered and vanished. All rose to go, obviously disgusted with what they have just heard. Here it was: Willner was turning into a dictator, all too soon, the one who planned to design every movement of each member of the crew, as if he were in army. The military drill seemed inevitable.

"It sounds worse than the army!" murmured Ian Callum buoyantly. "What is he thinking?"

"That he is a captain," O' Leary retorted. "He is responsible for us, for every single unit. He is not here to befriend us, he is to be a tough father with the whip in his hand. You will appreciate it in time."

Etta was following the captain with her eyes. What was he thinking? He had to manage the crew in five separate ships, showing no signs of weakness no matter what would happen. And people were allowed to sneer behind his back, but at the same time they had to count on him, trust him.

'*It is beyond the abilities of an ordinary man,*' she thought, feeling the urge to follow him, to tell him that he had her support, but the idea was more than inappropriate. And what was even worse, she liked the captain, liked him as a man. She sighed silently and dragged herself to her room.

Doctor O'Leary was standing in the corridor, looking at the holographic picture on the wall. Looking at the waterfall and the trees heaving in the breeze, one could almost smell the green.

"What do you think about the whole situation, sir?" she asked.

"My name is MacLean," he answered, looking at her in the corner of his eye. "Let's drop those formal titles, shall we? T would be only awkward in our situation. What do I think...? I think that our captain really tries to keep the gold of it. He tries to protect us from breaking down. But I wonder what happens if-"

"If he doesn't succeed?"

"No, kiddo. If he breaks first."

"Sir, do you really... You really think it is likely to happen?"

"And why would it be unlikely? He is just a human, like the rest of us. And as we all he has his own braking point."

"Let's hope he hasn't."

"Let's. He was chosen for a captain for a reason." O'Leary looked at Etta with his huge, watery eyes. It was not the first time that she thought they do not match his sarcasm and dark humor of the elderly scientist: they were wise, mild and unbearably sad.

"We'll see what happens in time. We have all the time in the world..." he concluded, the air of despair in his voice.

During the following weeks, the drill ordered by the captain seemed to be the only thing that would prevent people from suffering the claustrophobic moods. All of them suffered from it, stuffed in limited private and social space. Keeping together helped them to restrain their nerves and they ceased to treat it as a punishment or enslavement. The work-out help them to keep fit, the discussions and lectures made their minds drift away from their situation but for a moment. The machines and computers had to be checked every couple of hours, the temperature of the outer shell controlled, water collectors supervised. The capsules with the hibernated people inside were the apple of everybody's eye. There was no time to rest, no time for unnecessary emotions. The psychotherapy sessions that were being held weekly were a relief for everyone, as one could say anything during them, with no consequences at all. And nobody could show offense, even if criticized for no reason. The sessions were usually almost like battlefields, but once the quarrel was over, the whole matter was forgotten. The emotions sizzled and faded, but what was more important, those sessions were so home-like that they helped them forget where they were and where they were heading.

After two months of the journeys the crafts were nick-named "those damned cans", and a special schedule of distributing sedatives had to be made. *Hysteriae cosmicae,* aka space neurosis was more dangerous than anyone on the Earth could have expected. The realization of the frailty of the barrier separating the crew from the deadly vacuum outside was fueling the neurosis symptoms. The results of the mass hysteria could result in putting everyone in mortal danger.

The androids turned out to be of great help. They adapted quickly and learned how to maintain the craft systems. Leonard Derkacz was the one who put their new role into consideration and he oversaw the project and the androids' supervision. Some mean voices could be heard that he was not so different from the droid himself, and that was why he was getting along with them so well. After the droids' indoctrination Mission turned out to be successful, Derkacz sat into the ferry to go to remaining crafts and introduce his solution there, Raina at his side, as always, like if she were his shadow.

"I cannot get one thing: why cannot they update themselves?" asked Ian Callum during one of the lectures about the androids. "Cannot they just plug in to the computer?"

"It doesn't work like that," answered O'Leary, who was lecturing. "Just imbibing the data doesn't guarantee their proper interpretation. That is why the androids must learn and be supervised while doing so. If they had misinterpreted anything, we would all pay for that."

"Interpretation, that's the clue here. How can an artificial mind interpret anything?" asked doctor Xiao.

MacLean O' Leary found the proper illustration in his pad and projected it on the screen. It looked like a flattened sphere made of spirally twisted tiny-braid net.

"What you see here is an android's brain, the construction called 'the snail,' he started. "All the elements: logic circuits, steering processors, databanks, they are all put together into a three-dimensional, net-like construction that is placed into the droid's skull. Of course, the elements cannot touch one another. They are being manually placed to create the proper place for even spread of personality, if I can name it like that. Then the outer stimuli sensors are connected. One must be extra careful with the touch and pressure sensors, because the error here can cause the malfunction of the whole unit. When the robot is assembled, the skull is filled with chemo-gel, the ingredients of which are top-secret. It is the modified version of the bio-gel that was used in the past. The gel condensates into synapses and dendrites that links the systems and enables stimuli to cruise throughout the system. And only the minimal differences in the placing of the stall elements causes the differences in the droids personalities." He pointed to one of the elements of the construction. "Here is the sex-awareness center. When the simple household droids were being constructed, this area was completely ignored. The engineers had thought that the external masculine or feminine attributes would be enough for the droid to recognize its sexual identity. While the Companions gained the self-awareness, the processor that would enable them to identify with a given sex had to be developed. To keep the matter simple: female android knows she is a woman. It couldn't be made male by changing the outer attributes without causing some serious personality disturbance."

Callum, the biologist, raised his hand as if he were a mere schoolboy.

"Let's get back to the skin issue. How was the problem with pressure and heat sensors resolved?"

"I was to get back to that later but... The system works on the basis of the inner magnetic feedback. The artificial skin is the best insulator that was ever designed, but still, the outer magnetic field of two Teslas can disturb the work of sensors, even di-regulate them completely."

"That's interesting," murmured Callum. "Does it apply to different systems as well?"

"No, only pressure sensors. The temperature sensors in fingertips and earlobes are similar to the probers of electric current voltage. The droids had been equipped with one more extra sense, and that is the radiast, the ability to sense the radiation. Humans don't have it, because evolution decided it was useless for us."

"The sight and the hearing are obvious," doctor Xiao disrupted, "but what about the ear labyrinth? Is it a gyroscope?"

"Partially. In case of malfunction there is another system, the sonar. It can also replace the sight if it is gone for some reasons. Well, the androids surpass us in many matters. They were designed to lack the drawbacks of human body. Let's talk about the motoric system, shall we? The bones are made of titanium and some carbon compounds. It matches human skeleton, as it is the most sophisticated..."

Etta was listening to the lecture keeping her eyes on O'Leary. She had tried to infuse some knowledge about the Companions functioning and anatomy, but the Andropology books she had read were full of graphs and formulas she couldn't comprehend. She was obviously lacking some basic knowledge of physics, chemistry and mathematics. She had a humanist mind and the Commission of Profile Assignment confirmed that, so she hadn't wasted her precious time to learn science. But O'Leary here was as if aware of that, he was talking in a way everyone could understand the complex issues of androids' anatomy. She had questions, but didn't want to disturb the flow of the lecture.

She sat at the doctor's table at the tea-time meal.

"That was a superb lecture," she said shyly, "We don't they teach all that in school? It's more interesting than sci-fi novels!"

Doctor's look was full of ironic indulgency. He was seasoning his food with some spices.

"They do," he replied, "but in science profiled schools. And you are a humanist, am I right?"

"Shouldn't we all have access to the same knowledge?"

"We should. And we have, in general. Nobody would have stopped you if you wanted to study science. But you would have to do it on your own. The government pays only for the optimum schooling program, which is to produce the unit of optimum efficiency, according to the predispositions of that unit. And they do not wish the student to focus on the issues which wouldn't compromise to those predispositions. Why would an engineer waste his time for studying history of the arts? Why would an artist waste his time for algebra?"

"It sounds right, but I feel I lack something." Etta was not even focusing on the taste of her food, if it had any. She was milling the information from the lecture.

"The schooling system is efficient and it makes human society work. Here we should rather broaden our horizons than narrow them."

"I had asked you once to teach me, do you remember? Have you analyzed the answers of the test you had put me through? Would I be good enough for your student?"

"Well, what can I say...? You lack some basics, but it can be made up. The test results are promising. You are not dumb, nor lazy. I guess I could give you a chance." He rubbed his rough chin, looking at Etta thoughtfully. "I cannot see why you wouldn't lecture the crew?" he added after a pause. "Most of us are scientists, not knowing much about history."

"Would they be interested?"

"And were you interested in androids' anatomy? History is important, and if the lecturer can seize the crowd... and I think it would be good for us, the star people, gain some knowledge about the society that prepared such a fate for us."

It made sense. It was tempting and opened new doors for the teacher.

MacLean O'Leary smiled, seeing the impression he had made. He put a spoonful of his disgusting meal between his lips.

IV

Raul, sitting at the lower bench of the bunk bed and fixing some small device, noticed Etta's thoughtfulness once she stepped into the door.

"Is anything wrong?" he asked.

"No. Why have you asked that question?"

"You don't talk much, lately. Raina suggested that you don't need me anymore."

"No! What made you think that?" Etta looked at her Companion and realized that she had really abandoned him some time ago. Willner's integration drill made her spend less time in the company of her droid, so he could really have some strange thoughts. "It's not like that, my dear Raul!" She sat next to him and took his hand. "You know the captain's orders they are of great importance. But my following them doesn't mean you are less important to me."

Raul was silent, not looking at her.

"What happens to the droid that becomes of no use for his Dominant...?" he asked, forcing the words out.

"I've never heard of a case like that," Etta ensured him. "And you, especially you, don't have to worry about that. You are really special to me, essential to my survival, I cannot imagine existing without you!"

"And if you gained a human companion?" he asked. "A husband? You would have to choose, me or him, and for sure he wouldn't let you keep me."

Etta touched his cheek. There was no answer for Raul's doubts. She was quite aware of the fact that no human man would tolerate the Companion around his wife. But the Companions lived with women with no chances for marriage. And it was the same with men. But Willner had stirred the matter once. A woman could marry, a man could take a wife. What would happen to the droid then? Would it be dismantled? Passed to another, like a second-hand vacuum cleaner?

"I don't know what would happen then. But I can promise you that it is the matter that doesn't consider you. I'm not getting married. I don't even want to do that."

"You like the captain. I know you do." Raul looked her in the eye. It was useless to realize that his eyes were just polymer balls with tiny tracking devices inside. There was something more about them than smooth shell, the lenses and some fibers, sending the images to the artificial brain. What was happening to that droid? Why was he so different from his kind? And was he, really?

"Yes, I like the captain I like many men. But it doesn't result in anything and you know quite well it is so. Where do those doubts come from?"

"Why have people equipped us like that?" Raul spat out. "Why can't we be loyal to humankind? Why do we have to demand the company of one person?"

"Demand?" Etta repeated. "You mean crave?"

She was silent, shocked by her Companion's words. Raul was outstanding the frames of his programming. He was asking questions she wasn't prepared to answer. She was speechless, unless some noise behind her back made her turn her head around. O'Leary was standing in the door frame, holding her personal pod in his hand. She must have left it on the canteen table. The doctor was looking at Raul with his tired, watery eyes, and no tinge of surprise blemished his sight.

"Raul, the android. People hadn't equipped you with those systems," he said quietly. "You develop them on your own. But you are right in the matter that creating the A.I. that works beyond the Gonzaga Point is a one-way ticket."

'The Gonzaga Point' was the IQ border beyond which the artificial mind started to think on its own and make independent decisions. Professor Victor Emmanuelo Gonzaga calculated it in the year 325 of the New Era. It was all written in the second chapter of *Andropology*. Etta whispered the formula in her mind.

"It turns out that emotions don't have to be chemically stimulated, as it was once thought," O'Leary continued. "They are self-created beyond the Gonzaga Point, as if they were natural for the higher minds. And how exactly they develop hasn't been tested yet, it is a brand-new phenomenon, thought impossible before…" He stepped forward and placed Etta's pod on the table. "The dependence upon one Dominant is the mechanism that is not yet analyzed, but it is definitely real. There isn't a pattern in the original program, which would cause it to work. And believe me, Raul, we are not deliberately cruel towards you. We had dogs and cats as pets before you, but creating the prototype of the Companion was a milestone for humankind. Lonely people have somebody now they can talk to, they can interact with. Even the cutest and most submissive pet wasn't able to talk back, and the androids not only answered questions, but could react to word, could learn and think on its own. That was the main assumption. Otherwise we could produce clockwork hurdy-gurdies."

"The only purpose for our existence is to serve you."

"No. You got it wrong. You exist because we need you. It's the same with a baby that is born, because somebody awaits it. You save people from depression, from suicide, and not only that. Haven't you figured out that the presence of droids is the only guarantee of our getting to the destination?"

Raul lowered his head. He was milling the data, confronting them with conclusions he formed before.

"Why is it the only guarantee?" he asked finally.

"Cause you could help us in extreme situations," answered the doctor. "You wouldn't lose your temper, keep the cool blood. Well, it's a euphemism in your case, but you know what I mean for sure. Companions have always been loyal and helpful. You are mentally resistant, persistent, you cannot go crazy. I trust androids more than they trust themselves."

Raul looked at the Irishman, who was calm as a rock, as usual. And then the droid smiled faintly. And even though the grimace was mechanically induced, there was a spark in his eyes, as if he was really a human being.

"Thank you, doctor." He whispered.

Etta got really excited about the idea of being a teacher again. The situation was somewhat different: she was to lecture educated adults now, and not little kids. The captain accepted her draft entitled *Short introduction to the latest history.* Her anxiety had no real basis, all of the listeners: those physically present and those on-line, listened to her with curiosity that could have been compared to little kids'. And the doctor was right – most of them had heard the information she provided for the very first time.

"If it was not the junta, the complete chaos would flood the Earth in the first years after the eco-catastrophe. Despite the mass protests the military way of governing the people prevented the disorganization of countries. The situation was a precedence in the humankind history. It was first time that people started lacking food, globally. It was vanishing so fast that not even cutting it into small ratios was possible. To avoid global famine, the Cambodia system was introduced everywhere: all people, no matter what their material status was, were to be given the same food ratios. If one wanted to eat, one had to go to a canteen and collect the food there. Only the ones who were too sick or too old to get to the food point were taken to the special lazarettos where they could be taken care of. Cambodia had been associated with the bloody regime, so the idea of using the solutions from that country caused riots in the streets. They were nevertheless quite brutally extinguished and the system was finally introduced. One couldn't own any extra food, the only exception from that rule was so called additive, and that was the ratio of four to six lyophilized protein bars that every person was to carry. Some robberies that occurred to steal those extra ratios were quickly eliminated. Vegetables, fruit and meats were unavailable for a common citizen. To preserve as much nutrients as possible all the food was turned into a tasteless lyophilizates and of course there were many who didn't like that. The richest tried to take over the natural products or gain access to more ratios. The army reacted immediately, creating laws that resulted in confiscating the wealth or even public executions of the instigators. The rich had to come to terms with the realization that they won't get any better food than the middle and working class. The next controversial order was to euthanize all pets. Only the small percentage hidden by the richest and the most influential citizens survived, but as it was the matter of survival of the humankind, the order was mercilessly executed. The loss of the beloved pet was a personal tragedy for many. At that time, also the first program of genetic improvement was introduced."

"You need to realize that the freedom of breeding was as obvious for people as breathing. The introduction of the breeding laws cause riots as fierce as the mass nutrition campaign. People couldn't understand the need to produce just the strongest and the healthiest babies. It was more important that sustaining the individual and egoistic need to pass one's own genes, even poor ones. Even the Natural Selection Episode that took place right after the catastrophe and eliminated the weaker units, hadn't taught them anything.

"Excuse me, what was that episode, exactly?" engineer Woznansky asked.

"The lack of special food products and natural ingredients-based medicine caused global deaths among people terminally ill, with weak immune system and needing overall treatment, "Etta explained, "But luckily the gloomy scenario of anti-utopists, and that was mass-murder of people who were of no use for the society, didn't happen. On the contrary, people defended the members of their families who were too weak or too old to work.

Getting rid of such people was a narrow margin. But the lack of medicine and diet products was enough to eliminate them. Only those who could adapt to the changing environment survived. They were genetically tough, as it was said in those days. Of course, doctors did what they could to keep those who thrived healthy, but the number of those who were already sick, or were born sick and couldn't be saved, was increasing."

Etta stopped.

The physics, the engineers, the chemists, all were looking at her. Curiosity made their faces look like the faces of children. The projectors from other crafts showed the same. The lectures had always made people gather, but that one seemed of some special importance for them. But Etta didn't feel like talking much of the dark ages, when the armed bands were attacking people in the streets and the soldiers were executing the law-breakers on the spot, not wasting time for trials. Those were the days when civilians and army split up forever. Even though people knew that soldiers were there to protect them, excluding the cases when they tried to break the law, the fear appeared. The times were really awful: food of no taste, and barely enough to keep one alive, the feeling of helplessness and despair when ones you loved died in front of you. Helpless doctors who could not do much with the technology, but lacking the natural resources. And it only got a little better with time. The monotonous diet nevertheless resulted in less cases of strokes, diabetes, circulatory disorders and tumors. People were made to move, to exercise. It was the first time that people who weren't living up to the standards of spending given time in the gym, were punished by taking the food ratios away. The method of forcing people to exercise was used as anti-depressant, but it turned out to be also good for the hearts. So, as the years passed, obese people were gone, cripples were gone. So, they were also good sides of the situation."

That was how the society of Earth Union was established, wasn't it? Human had paid such a high price for the thoughtlessness they had shown; today's peace and safety was splattered with the blood of yesterday. But it was all gone. Or wasn't it? Almost half of the planet was still contaminated, the oceans were sterile. Only the bacteria and some algae appeared in the salty waters not so long ago, so there were chances for the water ecosystem to develop again. But when...?

"For over a century the theft of deficit goods like food, natural medicine, and fresh water, meant a death sentence, no matter how old the thief was. The law treated everyone equally, even kids. As the years passed and the resources were suppler, the system of mass feeding could be changed into ratio system..."

The lecture resulted in the lively discussion, disturbed only by the signal announcing supper.

"We haven't finished, so I suggest we continue our discussion at the evening integration hour," Etta proposed and the crew applauded her.

They all gathered in the main room after the meal, the listeners from the remaining crafts also present online.

"Please, explain, why had people protested against the control of the genotype of the population," doctor Gongadze started from the screen. "They must have known then how important the strong genotype was..."

"The past of eugenic is very gloomy, doctor," Etta replied, "its beginning tainted with violence and some twisted ideas of the 'race of lords'. We know nowadays that there was no such thing as a race in case of *Homo sapiens*. There are only slight variations, according to the environment they were developing through the generations, but it has nothing to do with the genotype. But the person's position in the society used to be determined by the skin shade once, even more than the gradient of the breeding ability now. The purest were "the whites", then there were "the yellow", next were "the blacks" and the lower shade was "the tawny", called also "the Hindi". Interracial marriages were forbidden in some time of the history, thinking the offspring of those as of lower value. Hundreds of years must have passed to change that way of thinking. But the struggle to prove which type was the most valuable lasted till the day of the ecological catastrophe."

"What was that gloomy past you were talking about?" engineer Lucy Camarro from Viking 02 asked. She was black and it was the first time she had heard that if she were born a couple of decades later her genes might have been excluded, even before running any tests.

"There were some plans of exterminating whole ethnic groups, whole nations, to control the evolution of the humankind. The waste of talents and potential was unbelievable, not mentioning the tragedies of every single unit..."

Derkacz extended his hand.

"Excuse me, Miss Solis," he interrupted, "but please explain one issue, that remains illogical to me, even though I had some extra classes on humankind history. The medicine and biology in the twentieth century of so called "AC era", not mentioning the twenty-first century, was highly developed. How was it possible that the program of obligatory sterilization of units with defective genes, mental disorders or addictions wasn't introduced? Even the primary school pupils must have known that the genome defectiveness is likely to be passed through generations, and it is like a bomb! And nothing was being done about that. Why?"

"That's true, but it is a complex issue of historical, cultural and religious nature. People who proposed introducing such programs were treated as assailants, personal freedom was of great value then. They were pushed at the margin of the society, ostracized from their work environment if they were scientists. They were even murdered. The resistance was too strong to introduce any logical social reforms. We can assume that if they had been introduced in the twentieth century, the number of victims of the eco catastrophe would be lower. And the chaos after it would be easier to control."

"It is hard to believe in such mass dumbness!" Veronica Hornet shook her head and leaned her chin on the fist, as it was her usual gesture. "Our ancestors, as a whole, were tempting extinction!"

"Not only was that weird then," said Colonel Steve Borden from Viking 05, the lawyer. "The civil law was constructed so it was more indulgent for criminals than for lawful citizens. I sometimes wonder how it was even possible that humankind survived!"

"They were breeding like rabbits, that's how!" O'Leary sneered.

"Yes, but considering the types of genes that were re-duplicated most often-"

"And I'd like to know why they allowed people to breed traditionally!" Woznansky dropped in. "In vitro is more efficient and allows to eliminate most of defects!"

"It is not always so," Xiao negated. "You think that they hadn't tried that? First of all, the costs of introducing and sustaining such program would consume ten percent of the country budget, and that is a barrier not easy to ignore. Then there are costs of hormonal therapy essential to keep the artificially planted fetus in the womb. Hormones can seriously affect mother's health, and the effects of such treatment are impossible to foresee. And if we are talking billions of eggs, the statistical spread of defects cannot be even predicted. The ten-year trial program proved, that one quarter of the babies conceived with the high-quality and pure genetic material were born with serious defects the scientists haven't even predicted."

"And those were...?"

"Mostly tumors, mainly liver tumors, epilepsy and the immune system disorders. The causes of that are not known, but the most possible theory points the differences in genotypes of mother and fetus. And there were also some psychological issues... So, finally, in vitro was performed only in cases when the gametes were obtained from the future parents and purified before the conception. But even that is not a guarantee of success. After the centuries of research, we do not know everything. And those psychological side effects..."

"What side effects?" Callum asked. "Mothers didn't love enough the babies that were genetically alien to them?"

Xiao shrugged her shoulders. She wasn't a psychologist, nevertheless she tried to explain the matter.

"Not necessarily. But in many cases the parents didn't feel the bond with the child, or the bond was loosened as the years passed and the baby turned out to be nothing like them. And the children reacted to that kind of forced love by developing various mental disorders. So, even though the followers of in vitro eugenic tried hard, it turned out that the natural breeding was the most efficient. Of course, genotype control was being maintained still."

The discussion lasted till the late hours and only the evening curfew roll call broke it.

Lying in her bed Etta thought that perhaps she would have to lecture the crew more than once, since they were so engaged in the topic.

And it was a nice realization, really nice.

V

The third month of the journey brought some unexpected trouble.

One evening Roger 7E discovered the opened circuit in the atomic reactor in the machine room of Viking 05. He closed it and enlisted the fault. The thorough investigation proved it to be just an oversight, but the fact that it had occurred was disturbing for everyone. Doctor Gongadze ordered the extra examination of the mental condition of all the members of the crew, but it proved everyone quite stable. The thorough examination of the crafts also proved everything worked perfectly. The algae cultivation system was almost ready to gather the first crops that were to enrich the menu, and the outer water collectors were performing better than anyone had expected. The minerals for enriching it were supplemented.

Sometime later, when everyone almost forgot the incident, a lot more disturbing accident happened during the lecture of Callum. The biologist was presenting the long forgotten "genetic immortality project" which was unknown to most of the crew.

"The assumptions of the project were really simple," Callum was explaining. "The use of the enzyme, telomerase, increases the life span of cells twice. Calories, when dosed precisely to increase the 'cell hunger', make mice live longer. Those are simple and effective therapies. So, why can't the gene responsible for aging and degeneration be isolated and switched off? Well, it actually can. But the euphoria of that discovery turned into dread after some more research. The experiments with *Drosopfila melanogaster* flies were bringing up some disturbing results. Once one simple gene responsible for the eye color was relocated, caused some schizophrenic behavior in adult specimen. They behaved irrationally. But the public opinion was sure that if we can fix the genes that had faults, we can also change them or replace them with others. Nothing farther from the truth."

"And why is that so?" Aisha Bahrani asked.

"The discovery was made not so long ago. The scientists could only suspect it was somewhere there, but the scientific apparatus was not precise enough to show it. And this is how it works: all of genes are tightly bound. They are irreplaceable in pairs, in threes, but sometimes the whole long chains just cannot be messed up with. And the aging gene relates to every other gene."

"If so couldn't it just be switched off?" The disappointment in the voice of Shamir Om, the chief engineer of Viking 05, was clearly audible.

"It could, but the results were horrible. Physical discomfort, monstrosities, various neurological and mental distortions. All those anomalies led the experiment to its finish."

"It's better that way," Warens, the technician from Viking 03, murmured. "Eternal life, what kind of idea is that?"

"Wouldn't you like to live longer?" O'Leary asked him.

There was no malice in his voice, no irony or mockery, but the technician reacted violently to that question, as if he were slapped in the face. He jumped up, pushing his chair to the floor at its side.

"Humans do not deserve immortality!" he shouted. "It would be given then if they deserved it, do you hear me? We aren't meant to live forever, we are to grow old and die, and because that's the only way the Earth could get rid of us one day! We are heading for the stars as if there were some creatures there awaiting us with their arms wide open! But they don't want us there, I am sure of that!" His voice broke into sobbing. "All of you, mark my words, none of us will survive this journey!"

Doctor Kenneth Linde pushed through to calm the hysterical ma down, but the mechanic became furious. It took few soldiers and a huge dose of sedative to put the man down.

"Take him to the diagnostic room and tie him to the bed." The doctor regained some control over the situation. "I'll see what I can do about it."

The travelers were overwhelmed by the episode. John Warens seemed to be calm and levelled, his sudden break down was a great surprise for the co-workers.

"I find nothing surprising in Warens behavior," O'Leary stated at the commanders' meeting. "I'm just surprised that it took such a long time for the first incident to occur."

"And what can you know about it? You are specializing in A.I, not in people!" Tengiz Gongadze barked.

"One must get to know human minds first, before programming and developing artificial brains," answered the Irishman calmly. "I've studied psychiatry and sociology, Andrology is my third specialization. The knowledge of human psyche and physiology is essential in my profession."

"And what does that knowledge of yours tell you?"

"The same it tells you, and all the doctors on board. Humans were not trained for such challenges on their path of evolution. Do you recall the underwater cities? After the first phase of awe over that 'splendid civilization milestone' all of the inhabitants were running away, even though the structures were highly comfortable."

"But we have no place to run now, we must get through it," the captain concluded. "What is the patient's condition, doctor?"

The chief doctor from Viking 03 grimaced briefly. His fair hair and youngish, smooth face made him look immature and Gongadze was highly surprised that such an inexperienced person got one of the most important positions on board. He remained silent, though.

"I will get him out of that," Linde assured. "It will take some time, but I have all the medicine and machines here."

"And if we are talking about machinery: who has claimed his spot in the engine room?"

"No one has," commander Kaori replied. "We have switched to technical droids. And I suggest you all to do the same."

TAs – Technical Androids, were more of simple robots than Companion Androids, which were called CAs. They were maintaining control over the right functioning of machinery and stability of outer shell. They had some freedom of choice and decisiveness. They were anthropomorphic, but one glimpse of an eye was enough to recognize they were not humans: their faces were blank, almost devoid of facial features, they were also wigless, which helped to keep them clean, as they often performed some 'dirty' jobs. They were helpful in many areas as technicians, but their IQ was low and could not be developed. And they must have been overseen while working. So even though they were called androids, it was only because of their seeming resemblance to humans. They were more of simple machines, really, devoid of thoughts and easy to program.

There were five TCs for each Viking. They remained deactivated so far, resting as some extra laborers, which could be used in case of emergency. Chief engineers were not happy with the idea of working with TAs, they preferred working with humans.

"Was any of you allowed to speak!?" Captain Willner shouted. "Commander Kaori is right, we need support and I will have none discussion in that matter! The Companions were performing the roles so far but they were not meant for it! Activate the TAs teams and give them the orders. And from now on I want two reports: human and non-human. And the Companions are to be back to their Dominants matters."

"Finally, some wise orders..." O'Leary said under his breath and one could really hear the appreciation in his voice.

The captain seemingly realized that giving the droids too many tasks which included taking care of people could be devastating for longer period. It was better that the android was responsible for just one Dominant and his or her needs.

"It's good to be rid of those androids," Callum murmured. "If anyone asked me I would say they give me chills."

"What do you mean?" asked Veronica coarsely.

"I cannot stand the idea they will thrive once we all are gone..."

"Ian, please stop saying nonsense," Derkacz sounded patronizing. "You cannot blame the androids for the way they are constructed. And we cannot really say how long their life span is. Bit we already know that the environment influences them, so they do not have to live longer than us. Your jealousy is ridiculous!"

Callum glanced at him with an evil eye. He looked like he was about to burst, like Warens, but he restrained his temper.

"It is not me who is ridiculous!" he said. "You worship those animated puppets and think they are better than humans. But even your own Companion couldn't stand you!"

That was something Etta hasn't heard before, so she tuned her radar in. The android's lean face remained blank.

"I gave Reina the choice she deserved to make," he said calmly. "There was nothing more I could do for her."

"And you think a robot can decide about itself?"

"Intelligence, Ian, is sealed with the freedom of choice. Raina wasn't assembled for me. Her Dominant had just stolen her, and I have just fixed all that he had broken. I do not need a Companion, so I let her choose her Dominant. What is so shocking about that?"

"I wonder if my electric razor would express its wishes if I let you fix it…?" Callum just walked out, almost slamming the non-existent door.

Doctor Xiao rushed after him, her forehead frowned. She decided to step in before Callum would lose control. It was milder that Waren's, but could get even worse.

"Whom had Reina chosen?" Etta looked at Raul standing next to her, but she has already known he answer.

"The captain," said the droid quietly. "He seemed to be fond of her from the beginning."

Etta muffled a sigh. Somewhere deep inside her had some hopes that the captain would looked at her as if she were a woman, and not only his employee. But it was likely possible, wasn't it? The soldiers were too disciplined for relationships. The migration was a military action, soaked in army drill so deep that even the civilian's coordinator was a soldier. The colonists were not to know about that fact. And perhaps they had some suspicions?

The couples on board were matched long ago. It was impossible to live celibate for months, for years maybe. Nobody expected them to endure it. Those who had the Companion wouldn't have to look for a mate. But there were some, like Commander Cyra Lavell, who dated somebody from time to time, even though she had her own Companion. Even Etta met the handsome Jake Lockerby, but she knew the romance wouldn't be born out of those dates. She had Raul, hadn't she? And he was more than enough for her.

The young teacher thought often about her brothers, sleeping in the liquid-filled capsules on board of Viking 05. She hadn't managed to meet them before the launch. She couldn't guess their feeling about the whole situation. They had been ripped out of the environment they knew, thoroughly examined and put to sleep. What did they feel? What were they said? Nobody was eager to tell her that. She only hoped that after they got to Patris, or rather – if they get to Patris at all – Diogo and Nando would understand. And they wouldn't be mad at her. She was not the one to blame, was she? Her opinion in the matter wasn't taken into consideration.

O'Leary stood next to her, watching her closely. She stirred, noticing him, turned her face, slightly red suddenly, towards him.

"Why are you looking at me like that…?"

"I'm just wondering…"

"Wondering what?"

"Before we started, the psychologists were designing all the possible scenarios for the flight. One of the tasks was to enlist the candidates for mental breakdowns. And you were first on that list. And here we are…"

"Such prognoses are sometimes worthless, as you can see. Before the catastrophe had happened, the prognoses were in favor of those close to nature. They were seen as the survivors, because they knew how to find themselves in the primitive conditions. And the fate had laughed at them, and only the inhabitants of the most civilized and developed cities survived. The discipline and technology had helped them. The primitive tribes are extinct, and the weaker countries got imbibed by stronger neighbors."

O'Leary shrugged.

"You can name it a Darwinian evolution. Those who could adapt, survived. But it was not an adaptation to the environment, but to the swift changes in it. And those who were running away from civilization, had died in their dying habitats."

"Such tragedy…" Etta sighed. She recalled the historical volumes about the heroic tries of saving Indians from the Amazonian jungles or the inhabitants of Papua New Guinea, the crews combing dying Africa in search of the babies who thrived, so alike famine-stricken monkeys… "Not many survived," she whispered. "Just the youngest. The adults, even collected in time were unable to adapt to the city reality, they died of longing for their habitats, for nature and space. They couldn't live in post-apocalyptic regime."

"But they had tried, at least. Can you remember the post-apo visions of the writers? The animal level societies of beasts hovering in ruins or underground, people against people? And the reality turned out to be brighter."

"A little brighter, but it doesn't mean that everyone turned into an angel suddenly. There were many who thought refugees devoured their supplies, their space, and their oxygen. It was not so bright, believe me. The assaulting of the fugitives by the armed bandits were an everyday issue, before the police and army took to that matter."

The doctor sneered, but said nothing. Perhaps he was thinking about Ireland, the real one, the island where his family came from centuries earlier. It was deserted for generations, like most of Europe, but in each Irishman veins there cruised some longing for their long-lost Green Island.

"You think that those breakdowns will continue?" corporal Lockerby interrupted his thoughts. They were some distant relatives and the doctor's opinions meant more for the young man than the opinions of medics and psychologists.

O'Leary just shrugged his shoulders.

"It's almost sure. We are flying with two space units a month…"

"Space units? And what the heck is that?" the youth was a crude soldier, he wasn't taught astronomy in the past.

"Space unit is the average distance from the Earth to the Sun. You could learn something from time to time, Jake. Anyway, we have at least thirty space units to go. Cuiper's Belt is not round the corner. And the living space inside the ships is limited. Claustrophobia is likely to happen, as well as some other neuroses."

"Couldn't we just speed up a little? Our engines are supposed to be such damned technological miracles, at least I was said they were."

"We could, why not? We could gain at least half the light speed. But we all inside would be smashed to pulp, the outer shells turned into sieves by space rubble. We haven't got enough amortization for it, nor deflectors that would survive such speed..."

"But..."

Etta left the man to their discussion and went to see the captain who had vanished when they were disputing. He was sitting in his cabin, making some notes in his pod. Was it a report of the latest events? Etta looked around discreetly. The only difference in the captain's quarter was a desk, with magnetic holders for the pods crowding it. They couldn't have been shattered if the craft swung to a side suddenly.

"Looking for something, little one?" Kirk Willner asked affectionately, looking up from his report. "You look like you've lost something."

"No, I just..." Etta hesitated. "I have just noticed there aren't any windows, anywhere... I thought they were essential in every cabin, like in the movies and books..."

The captain put his pod away.

"Why would we need any portholes?" he asked. "What would we see through them? We seemingly stay motionless; the stars do not move at all. People would think we don't move at all, and that would cause a riot inside! The only place one can look out is the captain's bridge, and nobody except me and the pilots can step inside. Well, there are exceptional situations, like the launch, for example."

He was right, as usual, but Etta craved some peek outside, no matter what was really there. But if they weren't there, one could just sit and pretend they were in an experimental bio-sphere on earth, that they weren't going anywhere. Were they some who had really thought that? Etta didn't feel the need to self-deceive. She suddenly realized that she maintained her mental stability thanks to Raul. His presence, the knowledge he was always there, gave her the assurance that others lacked.

The captain stood up.

"Come to the deck," he said. "I've called Kovacs and Veronica, but you will be needed there also."

"As who?"

"As a chronicler. I want you to write down what I am about to say."

Etta was walking with the man, baffled. The corridors were narrow, seemed stuffy and claustrophobic, like bowels of a giant serpent. They passed two disputing technicians, security guards patrol and Raul, going somewhere accompanied by a TA. The difference between them was stunning: TA was short, petite and bald, with square, faceless head and an extra eye in the center of his forehead. It was not an eye, actually, but a torch that drew energy from the battery located in the place of a heart. TA could work in darkness, too.

"Raul, is anything wrong?" she asked, stopping.

"There is a malfunction in the electrical circuit in the kitchen reported, we are going to check it. A-3 doesn't know the plan of the corridors yet."

Etta nodded. The main difference between the robots and the TAs was the program: that of TAs was not covering all they had to do, so they needed to be explained the span of their responsibilities. After that had been done, they worked effectively until being given some other instructions.

The captain stopped at the bridge entrance and spoke to the microphone in the wall panel:

"Kirk Willner. Launch the procedure of opening the gate."

"Voice authorization complete. Please provide the numeric code." The automatic voice demanded.

"A-zero-one-zero-one-one."

"The numeric code confirmed. Welcome to the bridge, captain."

The doors slid to the sides with a hiss.

"Leave it open till colonel Kovacs and lieutenant Hornet arrive."

"Yes, sir."

Etta stepped into the bridge with a thumping heart. She hasn't been here from the moment they took off. Only the captain, some of his deputies and the pilots were allowed in here. Even though the captain's orders were always the most important, he hasn't tried to mess with their job, since they had been schooled for a given job since they were little kids. They were the most respected members of the crew, they were treated as aristocracy. And they deserved it, as only ones who could hopefully bring the journey to its happy end.

The clear panel was separating the pilots' cockpit from the space of the bridge; the pilots – Amal Casimir and de Bernal - alarmed by some sound inaudible for the rest of the crew, stood up and saluted the commander. The nodded to Etta and went back to their work. Etta looked around hesitantly and finally peered through the main windscreen, at the distant stars, galaxies and constellations.

"It really looks like we aren't moving at all!" she whispered.

The captain patted her shoulder and pointed to the monitor of the steering control. One could see the curve of acceleration and the number of miles that had covered, increasing with absurd haste.

"You can see now why we are better without the portholes…" he said seriously.

Lieutenat Kovacs and Veronica arrived a couple of minutes later and the captain wasn't happy about that, looking at them angrily.

"Sorry for being late, captain, we were checking the malfunction in the kitchen, sir," Kovacs reported.

"And since when you are in the mechanics crew, lieutenant? And you, Miss Hornet?"

"It was sabotage, sir!" Veronica explained.

The captain's eyes darkened, his forehead frowned. He rubbed at his lips with his thumb and walked slowly across the bridge, to his seat.

"Report!" he demanded.

"The heating spiral has been partially cut. If Larson hadn't noticed that, the floor and walls panels might get electrified and many might have get electrocuted, and…" Kovacs hesitated.

"And what?"

"The water distillation system on Viking 04 was deliberately broken. That craft is cursed or something…? They are working on fixing it and gathering all the prints or whatever, but I don't think they would find any."

"Yes, I don't think so either." The captain nodded and rubbed his neck, he was visibly shaken and tried to gather his bearings. But when he finally spoke, his voice was levelled:

"A couple of hours ago the computer received a coded message meant only for me, but I want to share it with you. The chief of security and the civilian coordinator are definitely the people who should share the knowledge with me. And Miss Solis here, as a chronicler, should hear it from me, and not from the second hand. You are aware of the fact that the information is confidential. And that is why we are here, nothing can eavesdrop us here."

"The generals are still in touch with us, you know that, of course. What you may not be aware of is that there is an investigation back on earth in progress, the investigation on the Green October, the members of which were Dario Cantoralle and Professor Welles. They are deeply conspired, we have managed to arrest just a few pawns so far, minor members. One of them nevertheless informed the investigators that there are at least three saboteurs among our crew. So, we know that one of them is here, and one on Viking 04. But where are the others – that was impossible for the agents to sate."

"Excuse me, captain," Veronica interrupted, "but if anything happens, they may also die."

"And they know that. But those are fanatics. They think that if our Mission succeeds, human will abandon the Earth for good. And the best way to prevent that is making our Mission fail. They have that saying of their, I have it written somewhere…" He was searching his pod for a while and finally read aloud: "'All forces for the Earth, not the stars'. The leaders claim that the Earth can be saved, and if we waste the efforts for star cruises, we will condemn it do irreversible degradation."

"Why is it October?" Veronica asked. "Why isn't it May, or January?"

"It was in October when the government tried to launch the program of re-cultivation of the grounds ravaged by the contamination," Etta explained, "I've heard that some people named the month a symbol of the Earth re-birth. But I've never thought them to be extremists. I thought they were some organization like, you know, social club or something."

They were silent before Veronica said:

"I don't get it. Sabotaging the engine room, wouldn't that be obvious? The reactor explosion would damage other ships for sure, we stay close enough to one another."

"Yes, but they are not here to damage the ships, cause it would intensify the space program, it would make scientists increase the level of safety of space cruises. They rather want people to break. To prove, that humans are unable to go that far, that they cannot maintain their mental health," Kovacs said after a second thought. "I wonder, captain, if the saboteurs really are members of that idiotic organization?"

77

The captain looked at him, all curiosity.

"What do you mean?"

"Do you remember the event with Miss Solis? They tried to kidnap her, even though she is not the person who carries any vital information of the project. Even though the trap for her was set."

"And the conclusion is…?"

"I wonder who else had been assaulted while enjoying their pass. No one reported such thing, but it doesn't mean they didn't occur. Some members of the crew might have been brainwashed and they are not aware of they do now."

Captain Willner nodded approvingly. Maybe he thought likewise, because he wasn't surprised at all at the thought and didn't ask any questions.

Etta shrugged at the thought that her brothers had saved her from something really unpleasant.

"You think that was the case…?" she whispered.

The officer grimaced. He must have prepared the theory, because he couldn't stand the thought that there was a traitor among his men, even though that version was more probable that the fantastic story of brainwashing.

Kirk Willner sighed.

"We'll see," he said bitterly. "Until we catch those tricksters, we must be extremely careful. And not a word to any other members of the crew! I do not need any panic here."

VI

The explosion had seriously damaged the air-conditioning system.

The technicians estimated he time needed for fixing it for six days, and that meant the reserve air supply must be used. The fact caused some serious worry among the crew members.

This time the saboteur made a clear hit and used a very powerful explosive of new generation, and that brought a doom upon him. Following the trail of micro chemical tracks one of the security guards was caught. And it wasn't a surprise. It must have been a soldier, as they were the last link chosen for closing the chain of the crew. The rest of the crew were so thoroughly examined and prepared, that it would be impossible not to detect their extremist sympathies. The soldiers were thought to be verified by the army. And it turned out not to be enough of a verification.

The busted soldier, Buster MacBride – his name was a kind of laugh in the situation – was taken by the space ferry to Viking 01 only two hours after the investigation had started. He tried to deny at first, but when his guilt became obvious, his face turned into a hardened visage of a person all too sure of the rightness of his case.

"Do what you will," he said coldly. "I won't say anything. I would do it again if I had an opportunity."

"Why are they questioning him at all?" Etta asked Doctor O'Leary. "His blame is obvious!"

"Yes, but there are others at large. It would be good to know their plans, don't you think?"

Captain Willner had a short conversation with Tengiz Gongadze, who came aboard the main craft, but the man only turned his head no.

"Now they all know how to take precautions against this," he said.

"The captain intended to inject him some truth-serum…" Veronica murmured.

Kirk Willner looked at the prisoner thoughtfully for a long while.

"Why have you done that?" he asked mildly.

"I have my reasons!" the soldier barked.

"What are the reasons for killing the colonists, the crew and yourself?"

"I wanted us to turn back! We need to save our planet, and not waste money and resources for some fairy tales!"

"It's all a point of view." Willner was looking at him with those calm, blue eyes, as if he sympathized with the man. "We know you are not the only one. And those attempts of yours are not all you can do, am I right?"

"Course they aren't! You'll see soon what we are capable of! You'll have to turn back!"

"What is it you're planning?"

"I won't tell you a damned word! You will all see that you should have stayed put of earth!"

The gathered crew shuddered. The voice of the soldier was fanatically tough, full of menace, it was not easy to remain untouched by it.

"Are you aware that you've earned a death sentence?" Kovacs asked, and MacBride just laughed despitefully.

"I may be gone, but the Earth will survive!"

"Are you even listening to the rubbish you say? Tell whatever you know, until you are still alive!" doctor Xiao shouted.

The soldier just gestured towards here explicitly and added some vulgar comment that made everybody sure he wouldn't speak against his sect.

"Be wise, MacBride! The captain would sure spare you, if you speak." Leonid Derkacz was as helpless as anyone else.

The young private was triumphant. The international law convention was at his side, he could withhold his testimony. The law, both military and civil, was the law, and it was never broken.

"You tell me right now what you're planning!" shouted the captain, he had clearly enough of that circus.

"I will tell you nothing, and when we return, I will sue all of you!" the soldier retorted. "It is pestering the captive, what you all are doing here, and there is a paragraph for that!"

"He's right..." O'Leary grumbled.

"What...?" Veronica gasped.

"That's true, Miss Hornet. I know the law he's quoting here, and it is the law that applies even in space, doesn't it?"

"Do something with that man, because..." Captain hasn't finished.

O'Leary was about to speak, and Veronica was munching some curse, when somebody pushed through the crowd. It was Raina, and she approached MacBride swiftly.

"The captain ordered you to answer!" she said in her levelled voice.

'Tone zero one, affirmative' thought Etta automatically.

"And what is that to you, dolly?" the private sneered.

"Please, answer."

"Not in the world, and get your ass out of here, before I kick you so hard that all of your screws will."

He hasn't managed to finish, the android grabbed his hand and twisted his fingers, so the man shrieked and fell to his knees. The droid's face remained poker, her voice levelled as before.

"The captain asked you something."

"Let go…!"

"Please, answer."

"The main computer, the virus! That is all I know! We were to focus your attention, so that the virus wouldn't be detected! Take that robot away, I'm begging you!"

"Raina, stop it!" the captain has just regained some control over his voice.

It all happened so fast, that not only the captain couldn't think of any reaction to the situation.

The android let her victim go, the man moaned painfully and collapsed to the floor.

"Get this rat out of here!" Willner ordered, embracing his Companion. "Easy, little one, easy…!" He was looking at her considerately.

Raina was motionless, her eyes empty, as if she hasn't even heard his words. Derkacz moved the captain away and flashed a small torch into her pupils.

"Why have you done that?" he asked.

"Misbehavior. Punishment. It's necessary. The one who misbehaved is punished."

"And what makes you think like that?"

"I don't think, I know. There is just one dominant in the house. Punishment always has a cause. No cause, no punishment."

"They must be the words of her first dominant. She must have remembered them," O'Leary concluded. "Nobody had cancelled his orders, so she thinks they are valid. Come on, people, nothing so serious has just happened!"

"That's some interesting conclusion," Kovacks sneered.

Gongadze and Xiao were attending to the soldier's hand. He ceased to moan, but all of his buoyant stamina was gone.

"He's all right," Gongadze said. "She knew what she was doing. Doctor Derkacz, is that droid dangerous? I need to know what to expect as a chief doctor!"

"Raina is not dangerous at all." Leonid put a torch into his pocket. "She just needs a lesson in the human rights. I admit, I haven't thought of that. She had witnessed too much violence in the period of shaping her consciousness. And she decided that it works everywhere and always."

Etta shrugged. She had suspected Dario to abuse her sister, but she hoped those were her illusions. But if he really assaulted his family, why had Nayeli defended him? She couldn't grasp that.

Etta sneaked out of the room. She was shattered by the situation and didn't want anyone to know that. She hated the ship all of a sudden, she longed for a walk in the park, for grocery shopping, for the view out of her window. She wanted to take a real bath so much, and not to be forced to stand for a quarter in the ozone tube, where she had to put an oxygen mask and wait for ozone winds to clean the dirt particles away. Her only dream now was a simple bath! People were not talking about that, but they would sacrifice a year of their lives to waste some precious water away in the shower! Everybody wasted some of their daily portion of water to wash the face or some other delicate body parts, and it had a thrill of a crime. Etta had enough of the cruise, and the situation with Raina made the journey even more unbearable. She had never witnessed anything so violent. She almost run to her cabin to cry silently into her pillow, hoping the tears would wash away her emotions.

Raul was there. He was tidying the interior, smoothing the sheets, arranging the items, the only thing Missing was a dust feather in his hand, but there was no dust in space. But he was dusting the shelves with some cloth anyway.

He looked at Etta, cocking his head in silent question.

"Don't say a word!" the girl stopped him before he uttered it. "Just hold me, hold me tight!"

He didn't have to understand, but he obeyed her, holding her close to his seemingly muscular chest.

'That's so weird...' Etta thought. "He is not a human, he doesn't breath, his heart doesn't beat, and nevertheless I find peace in his arms..."

Captain Willner was sitting in his room, finishing the report he was about to send to the headquarters on earth. He has described briefly what had happened and what has been done about the situation. And he's done a lot. The whole convoy was stopped, the crew examined and the past of each member checked once again in detail. But only a trap set for the saboteurs allowed him to catch two more, one on Viking 04, the other on board of Viking 05. The remaining ships seemed to be clear, nevertheless they were searched thoroughly once more. The soldiers were not happy about all that, because it was their group that was the most suspicious. Some of them felt personally offended.

All the technicians were scanning the crafts' computer net in search of the virus. The rest of the crew were sniffing through the crafts, paying closest attention to the less visited parts. O'Leary was laughing bitterly, saying that the whole control department on the Earth should perform seppuku. And as nobody on the crew knew what the heck seppuku was, he had to explain that he had meant the ritual suicide. Each craft had some explosives ready to be set, and not one, but six different viruses were detected in the computer system. And the I.Ts suspected there could be more of them.

"Let's ask Raina to question our prisoners, I wonder what she would drag out of them!" Kovacks proposed.

"Enough, Imre!" the captain barked and focused his attention on Stiepan Pavlov, the chief computer technician, who was online. "How long are you going to mess with the system?"

"You mean clearing the system or diagnosing the viruses?"

"Both."

"The system needs a re-start. We need a couple of hours, well, maybe a day to run all of the tests. The viruses were uploaded to a portable computer, not connected to our network, so we can analyze them as long as we wish. They are masterpieces, whomever had designed them, didn't lack resources, craft and imagination."

Pavlov was obviously in awe of the hackers' skills, even though they caused him so much trouble. The convoy system could be cleared quite fast and efficiently, but the viruses seemed so complex that he couldn't figure them out. After a couple of days work the computer technicians agreed that they were to be activated by some complex number configuration, and not a direct order from a man.

"They were to stop us once we were at a given distance from the earth, and made us go back." Derkacz concluded.

"Stop us, I can get that. But how could they make us go back? We would manage to restart the system, wouldn't we?" Doubted engineer Woznansky.

"Not necessarily. One of the viruses I've managed to deconstruct was to take over the steering and make the trip data into an invective mode."

"What...?"

"Sorry, an Andropology jargon... a mirror mode."

The constructors and specialists on android brains were Andropologist, but they were still messed with anthropologists in discussion...

"A mirror mode? You mean inverted?"

"Exactly. We would still think we were heading for Cuiper's Belt, while in reality we would go back and head towards the Earth."

"Oh… What a surprise we would have at getting to the destination…!"

"Lieutenant Denberry reported one of the bombs in the capsules compartments." Kovacks interrupted. "Isn't that an attempted murder?"

The captain frowned, switched on the communication panel and called Viking 04.

"I'm calling Danberry…"

The panel flashed and the hologram of the young, uniformed soldier appeared.

"Sir!" he was speaking nice, deep baritone.

"What would be the damage caused by the bomb you had found in passengers' compartment?"

"The automatic control system and monitoring would be gone. We would have to wake them all up, and that would equal disaster. We haven't got neither the place for them, nor the supplies."

The captain considered his words, then switched the conference mode.

"Attention all crafts! All the commanders meet me at the main deck at four p. m.! In person! It's a matter of the highest priority. Over and out!"

All the crafts confirmed, and then the communicator went silent. Kovacks also confirmed, only to be ordered:

"Inform Solis and Hornet. They are to be here on time."

"Yes, sir!"

Kovacks went out only to meet Etta almost at the threshold. He told her the captain's request and was off in search for Veronica.

Etta knocked at the door, surprised and uneasy.

"Enter!" Willer shouted and raised his eyebrows seeing the girl. "Is something wrong?"

"No... I mean...if it is the security guards meeting, what am I to do there?" she stuttered, intimidated by the captain's cold eyes.

"You are the chronicles. We need a witness," he said officially.

"The chronicler? So, am I to write everything down, or just what I decide important?"

Willner softened, even smiled a little.

"You ask my preferences?"

"Yes."

"Little one, I mean, Miss Solis, I cannot order you anything in that matter. You are beyond my command, I do not even have the right to look into your notes."

"But you are the captain..."

"...the first after God. Well, the times are different. I am not allowed to inquire into the chronicle. You write down whatever you think necessary. The Earth trusted you in that matter, they had chosen you as a person who is trustworthy and honest. I will be glad if you just simply write down the truth."

"Yes, sir!" Etta saluted, smiled and rushed out.

Keeping the diary of the trip was something really important for her. She often wondered how to put down an event without being judgmental, and staying as close to the truth as possible. The weird Reina's reaction was extremely problematic for her. It was a drudge, actually, she hasn't managed to write the final version till today. She decided to ask O'Leary for advice.

She turned into number four corridor, to the doctor's quarters. He dwelled with Leonid Derkacz for practical reasons: they were both developing some conceptual projects and could easily consult. O'Leary sat alone. Derkacz was in the engine room, where he was running some casual diagnostics of AT. The doctor was so deep in his computer calculations that he hadn't noticed Etta's knock at first. Only after she had banged harder did he exclaim something that could be read as an invitation to come in.

"Oh, it's you," he said to her. "Is there something wrong or did you come to sustain my playboy reputation?"

"Could you be serious, just this once?" Etta sighed. "I came for advice."

"What kind of advice?"

"I cannot put the Raina episode down. I want to note the truth, but I do not want her to look dangerous in my report. Somebody might draw wrong conclusions out of it."

O'Leary put the computer away and produced a small bottle made of plastone - a glass-like looking, feather-light material - out of the drawer.

"Let's drink," he proposed. "That will open some new perspectives."

"How did you manage to smuggle alcohol on board?!"

"I didn't have to smuggle anything! I just packed it into my hand luggage instead of some drags and trash. I put in some whiskey, gin and brandy. Oh, and some cognac, but that's for a special occasion!"

"That's an impressive portable bar! But it will dry out one day." Eta was looking with disapproval as the man was pouring the amber liquid into burets.

"That's why I'm a scientist. In Middle Ages every redneck could produce booze out of any weed, I will manage to do likewise here for sure! So, bottoms up!" O'Leary took a swallow and seated himself in front of Etta with the glass in his hand.

She also sipped. She felt like having something stronger for a while now.

"And of you ask me about Raina, I can tell you this: the problem with her is that she *is* dangerous. Perhaps the old man will tame her. Perhaps. Androids are more like people than you might think. They learn from examples, from their environment, like children but they lack the child's flexibility. What they experience in the first period of their functioning is scorched in their brains forever and it is really hard to change their way of thinking afterwards. Raina is convinced that violence can solve many problems. And the only thing that restraints her is the realization that her present Dominant is against violence. As long as she remembers that we can rest at peace. But in the non-conventional situation that sweet little girl can act likewise. And it is all because of your brother-in-law."

"You haven't told that to the captain and the security guards," Etta whispered.

"I told it to the captain. He must know what to expect. But none more. The guards would demand the deactivation, and that would be the simple execution of the potentially dangerous android. I don't want that. I believe that Raina will change her attitude in time. She only needs patience and tender care."

The doctor sipped some more and leaned his never properly shaved face towards the teacher. She could clearly see his bleached irises, red veins in the orbs, and that sadness, always there in his eyes, even when he was laughing and joking with others.

"I will tell you a secret, it is the Raina's issue that saved the saboteurs."

"What do you mean?"

"Kirk Willner would never show her that people, even the criminal, could be just killed, just like that. And then we are off to dinner after the execution. Nobody knows what would be the reaction to such knowledge in our Combat Girl."

"You really think so?"

"You will see in two hours."

"Have you been eavesdropping?"

"I like to be well informed."

Such behavior was astonishing, but it didn't surprise when O'Leary was involved. But Etta was somewhere else. She could still picture the delicate features of the android and her latte-colored face.

"It is not her fault," she whispered finally. "She just thinks that's how it goes."

"It is so. Good and evil are just a point of view. It is like hitting the child and saying that it is for its good. It will always think that love is expressed like that. Raina had never been loved, but she watched Dario abusing his family and explaining that it was for their good. I am sorry, I was not to tell you that..."

Etta sipped absentmindedly and coughed, the brandy was stronger than she had previously assumed.

"I figured that out myself. But why did Nayeli react so violently, instead of being happy that it was over?"

"The Stockholm Syndrome, my dear child. The oppressors know damn too well how to dominate the victim completely, especially if the victim is not too intelligent. And your sister will never realize what a great misfortune Dario Cantorale was for her."

Back in her room, Etta opened the register and rote down a paragraph:

The Android Raina forced the prisoner to confess, before anyone managed to stop her. As it turned out later, she had misinterpreted the Captains words. She didn't do any major harm to Buster MacBride. Doctor Leonid Derkacz obliged for correcting her way of thinking, which was distorted by the previous Dominant...

At the given time all the security chiefs: Denberry, Kovacs, Perez, Lavatto and Denham, gathered at the deck of Viking 01. Veronica and Etta were also there. The captain, with his usual aura of pristine peace, appeared the last.

"We are all gathered, as I can see," he started, "so please take your seats at the table. The officers here must have guessed the cause of our meeting here. We need to make some final decision about the fate of saboteurs."

"There are three of them, right?" asked colonel Lavatto from Viking 05.

"Right. We cannot keep them in cells, as they are supposed to be a temporary accommodation. And I just cannot imagine setting them free."

"So there is no place for a discussion here. Execution," Kovacs stated.

"Come, come!" Danberry disagreed. "None of them killed anyone. And it makes a lot of room for a discussion! Colonel Denham is a lawyer, as far as I am aware."

"I am also a lawyer," Kovacs interrupted. "So we could discuss and argument our right for ages. But it doesn't change the fact that those people are saboteurs and are a threat to the Mission!"

"And our priority is to keep the colonists safe," added lieutenant Perez. "Do I have to remind you that one of the bombs was found at the colonists' lair?"

Etta thought immediately about her brothers sleeping there. Would she be able to kill somebody who were a mortal danger to them? She realized with dread that she probably would. The ethics she had been fed with since she was a little girl was not as unquestionable as she previously assumed.

"We have disarmed all the bombs and no one was hurt," Carla Denham said. "Lieutenant Danberry is right, there is no paragraph that would allow us to put those people to death. We can imprison them, which would stand in collision with the Personal Rights Card."

"So the only solution left is lobotomy," said Lavatto.

"I object!" Veronica shouted. "It's worse than death!"

Lavatto shrugged her shoulders.

"Prison - wrong, death - wrong, lobotomy - wrong. There is always someone objecting! So, what are we supposed to do? Leave them on some passing asteroid?" she asked ironically.

The captain chimed his spoon on a metal mug, so everyone turned towards him.

"I was just about to propose something like that. We need to sacrifice one of the ferries and send the prisoners to Max Planck space station at Venus orbit. I have already talked to the commanders, they agreed to hold the saboteurs till the Earth sends someone to collect them."

"The ferry will not manage to get to Venus! We are far beyond the planet!" Perez doubted.

"It will not get to Venus, but it will get to the point where it will be intercepted by the craft sent from Planck. Camus de Bernal will set the cruise control so the risk of any collision is minimal," the captain explained. "Will we send the decoding key to the station, so they will be able to take control over the steers."

The officers looked at one another and whispered some remarks.

"It's not such a bad idea," Kovacs said. "They will not travel in comfortable way, but we don't need to take care of such scums! Losing a ferry is a pity, though. It will weaken our potential. I still think they should be simply executed."

"I agree, but we cannot get too emotional over the matter." Kirk Willner was playing absentmindedly with his pod. "Think about it, what would colonists say about it in some time? Or issue is too important to start it with a bloodshed."

"Exactly!" Veronica added. "We cannot make colonists fear the soldiers! The society does not trust the army. They need to trust me, as I am their coordinator, they need also trust the soldiers."

"We were not the ones who wanted a bloodbath."

"I know," the captain nodded. "But I think that my proposition is still better. Do you all accept it?"

The officers whispered again, Etta and Veronica exchanging uneasy glances. The captain did not cancel the execution option. If all the security chiefs voted for it... but fortunately they didn't.

"We agree to your proposition, captain," Kovacs said finally, "it really seems to be optimal."

"Miss Solis, note that all of the officers agreed to removing the saboteurs off the craft and placing them in the temporary custody of the Max Planck space station security guards." The captain turned to Etta. "I'm closing the meeting, please proceed with your duties."

"Let's hope that will end our trouble..." Veronica sighed with relief. Of course she wouldn't admit that, but the mere thought of sharing the enclosed space of the shaft with someone, who was ready to put in danger over a thousand people because of some sick ideals, made a cold shudder crawl down her spine.

VII

The unexpected short circuit on Viking 01 was unusual, as it cut down all the systems at once, leaving the craft dark and silent. The members of the crew hurled outside their cabins, torches in hands, trying to figure the situation out. The alarm lights were off, and it seemed that the system had been damaged earlier. The reports of AIs stated that the electric impulse couldn't have gotten into the emergency lightning system. Woznansky, evidently confused, and all of his men confirmed that.

"Why are you standing like that? Go fix it!" the captain scolded them.

He was so absorbed with the situation that he jumped out of his room wearing only underwear, so everybody could admire his body now. Even though he was quite stout and short, Etta's flashlight beam was sliding on his form shamelessly, and the girl thought he looked splendid. His muscles not too tense, strong and flex. Etta hated hairy men and noted with satisfaction that his chest, arms and legs were shaven. But why did she even care about his looks? He was sexy, that was more than obvious, and she had to admit that.

"Stop staring at him like that!" Veronica whispered merrily, appearing right at Etta's side. "Your Companions will became jealous in a moment!"

Etta looked at Raoul, then at Raina.

"Sure they would," she murmured, but at the same time felt a stab in her heart. She thought about Raul shaking Dario, even he was not ordered to do so. Androids shouldn't be able to feel jealousy, but as Etta was getting to know them better, she realized that the authors of *Andropology* had really no idea of how an android brain works. They knew only the mechanics, they could trace the changes in mnemonics. They could describe all that as technicians, but the inner life of AC remained a mystery to them. Or rather it would remain a mystery, if they even bothered to think about that. And they seemed not to care. The only thing they cared about was that ACs were not able to rebel.

Some muffled cursing came from the side corridor and Woznansky appeared, his path lighted by AT-4's third eye.

"Whoever did that, tried hard!" the engineer hissed. "We are blind, deaf and helpless!"

"What is broken?" the captain asked.

"Everything is broken! Nothing works!" Woznansky threw his arms up. "Lights, heating, air-conditioning systems, steering, communication, everything is dead!"

"Some overlooked virus?"

"Yes, but not in the main system. Something in the parallel wiring. I have some assumptions, but they will be confirmed when ATs get to the circuits. And the impulse that induced all that, it was something unknown, and for sure it wasn't generated by something in the power generators. They are all secured.

"The security systems might break."

"One maybe, but not all of them at the same time. Somebody had to plan it and start working on the sabotage after we had started, everything was all right at the final check-up."

"It means just one thing," the captain said slowly, "and that is that we haven't managed to catch all of the saboteurs. There is one more, at least one more, and here, at the main craft."

"Are you surprised? It is the most logical choice for the attack!" O'Leary yawned. He was standing next to Etta, wearing only his pajamas. He was barefoot, his face suggesting that there is just one thought in his mind, and that is to get back to bed. The situation couldn't crack his usual pessimism. His assistant seemed to be as calm, but judging by some little nervous gestures, he was more move than he wanted everybody to know.

"And why do gravity system work? We should fly like butterflies around here!" he asked.

"They are equipped in the independent energy-providing systems. The gravity system is a completely different mechanism. It is an autonomic magnet-pulse device, and it also creates the essential magnetosphere around the shaft. And it will continue even after we all suffocate here, like some rats trapped in the bottle!"

"Stop with that comparisons," the captain interrupted. "When will the oxygen saturation drop below the safe level?"

Ian Callum looked up, counting silently.

"In twelve hours. And the inner life-sustaining systems in the capsules maybe two hours longer."

"So at least we know how much time we have to fix it. Can we at least talk to the rest of the ships?" Willner asked.

"No, sir," Jimenez, the pilot, broke in. "And we cannot even see them, because the extra security systems had closed the blinds in the vision slots. All of the automatics and manual steering are blocked now." He sounded like a person who has just been robbed. The pilots thought about the bridge and the cockpit as if they owned it, as if they were parts of their bodies. They felt helpless without them, useless.

"So unblock them!" The captain frowned. "You were trained for that, as far as I am aware!"

"We cannot do anything without power."

"And the spare batteries?"

"They are in the storage. And the gate is shut. We cannot open it without power. It's the close circuit..."

"The main problem with civilization is that people get used to it all too easily! Human creativity died!" O'Leary barked. "Woznansky! Which circuit do we have to plug in to fix all the rest?"

"Of course the tool room. All the instruments are down, we are running on dead gear. As I said, somebody had planned if carefully."

"I don't give a damn about that rat's plan! Just be useful and mark the tools from the most to the least important."

"And what for?" The engineer threw O'Leary surprised glance, as if he had just noticed his shabby figure.

"Shit for! No you know what for? And now attention everyone! Bring all of you battery-charged devices to the conference room. Torches, razors, readers, palmtops, dildos, anything with batteries inside!" O'Leary scratched his flesh somewhere under his pajamas. "There is not a moment of peace on this damned boat!"

And as it turned out people trusted the old eccentric enough to bend to his command. The pile of electric gadgets collected in personal cabins rose in the conference room. O'Leary appeared back as one of the last, dragging some old-fashioned equipment the destination of which was unknown to all.

"That's the accumulator," he explained to the flabbergasted faces. "Something that is so old fashioned that everyone thinks I'm a lunatic when I ask for spare parts to it. I was assembling it in my spare time, just to relax a little. If we are lucky enough, I will manage to draw enough energy from those appliances to start the reactor's power reserve. And then we are down the hill!"

"Has anyone told you, you are a genius?" Etta asked, breaking the silence as all stared at him in amazement.

"Yes, some people has," he replied calmly, plugging a torch to his accumulator. "But you can repeat it once more, so all can remember that."

"And you are trying to start the reactor with... that?" Woznansky was looking at the massive cube, with clamps and some metal bars sticking out of it. The one who had assembled that hadn't cared about the aesthetics, the machine looked like dragged out of a heap of scrap before being melted in a furnace.

"I'm not trying, I'm going to do that, if I only manage to charge that thing. You should know better that others that I only need to start the self-charging valve, not the whole pyre. When the voltage is high enough that the aggregate sustains the cooling system, we will be able to start the whole pyre, with no risk at all. But the better idea is to charge the essential tools. Reactor won't start in few minutes, and before it does we would be able to do some minor fixes."

"You can lecture your own grandmother!" Woznansky barked. "If you can really help, then you deserve some appreciation, but save me that tone!"

O'Leary just smiled mockingly, still busy with his work.

"That's an interesting remark. Did you know that my grandmother could build a simple logic circuit with a chewing gum wrap, copper wire, a piece of plastic and a folding knife? At twenty-fife she was already a doctor of chemistry and physics? I don't think she would let anyone lecture her."

"Enough!" the captain interrupted. "Don't waste your stamina and wit for quarrels! Woznansky, why aren't you overseeing the repairs? You are not needed here."

"Ekhm... Yes, sir."

The chief engineer left the conference room with a sour face, trying to restrain his rage. He's never liked MacLean O'Leary, and now his loath went double. But Willner was right, he was needed more in the engine room, where ATs were trying to fix whatever they could. He was blind in the darkness, since he gave his torch to O'Leary. The layout of the ship was simple enough for everyone to memorize it.

He stepped into the engine room, the beams from AT head lights' slicing the gloom, and engineer Gudrun Silberstein stood up from the place she was kneeling. She was holding some small object, like a nugget of coal.

"Look at this, boss!" she said. "It is the same with every major joint."

Woznansky looked at the strange crumble he held in his fingers. It was burned, but it held its original shape. And he was more than sure that it was a timer detonator, usually used in the emergency circuit. And those were never installed with the important connections in the life-sustaining systems or in the engine room.

"Somebody had tried hard," he murmured.

"There's something more." Silberstain rubbed her hands on her overalls. "The first diagnostics we'd run wasn't thorough. The emergency air conditioning still works, and there is some minimal power imply in the passengers compartment."

"I wonder why? Didn't you find the detonator there?"

"We did. But it didn't come off."

"And do you know why?"

"Not yet. The break in the impulse igniting all of the bombs could take place in just one spot, and that is at the border between the passengers and crew compartments. I have been waiting for you to go there."

"Good. Let Kumar and Schroede proceed here and we go take a look. AT three, come with us!"

Little robot stopped whatever he was working on and joined the engineers. His third halogen eye was enlightening their path through the narrow corridor.

The passengers section was separated from the crew lodgings by double lock. It was necessary to keep the proper atmosphere in the passengers' room. There was no air there that could be breathable, but a mixture of compressed gasses that was a kind of air cushion protecting the fragile parts of the capsules. And there they were, adults and children alike, like pupas in their cocoons, sleeping the dreamless sleep, helpless, soaked in water spiced with some secret ingredients. The gasses were muffling any shocks and kept the temperature stable. It was also inflammable, so if any of the capsules would break and burn, others were safe. The designers had thought about everything.

The room with protective suit was attached to the main chamber, one could not do any maintenance or life-saving action without putting them on. It was a passage engineer Silberstein mentioned, leading to the bulkhead. Only the technicians were aware of the existence of that passage. Viking 01 harbored some secrets available only for those who needed such knowledge.

"Who's been in here?" Woznansky asked.

"Hard to tell. My scanner says that the door had been used, but it doesn't read the DNA codes. It's meant for diagnosing the machines. AI, give me some light."

The little robot stepped forward to point his torch into the small compartment. Both engineers were silent for a while, imbibing the view, finally Silberstein whispered:

"Oh my god, boss… How are we going to tell her about it?"

Nobody was prepared for such emotional reaction. Veronica was sobbing, screaming and throwing her arms in the air, as if she were an ancient mourner. She begged, whining:

"Brent! Speak up! Look at me! Say something! Don't die! What will I do without you? Brent!!"

"Stop screaming, for god's sakes!" doctor Xiao finally shouted, searching her bag for some sedative. "Your whiling will do no good here!"

"Breeeent!" the girl howled, kneeling over the still android, not listening to anyone around.

"And be so kind and stop calling the droids by human names!" The doctor's fuse was getting shorter, she grabbed her arm to inject the medicine. "He is branded Rasmus, Brent in a human name, not meant for a machine."

"He's not a machine, you puny shaman!" Veronica yelled and she barely restrained herself from slapping the petite Chinese.

"Nonsense!" Xiao sneered, putting the disposable injector into her bag. "We can all die here and she is whining over a broken toy!"

"You are the one who is broken!"

"Order!" demanded MacLean O'Leary, who has just appeared. "What kind of childish behavior is that? Like kids in the sandbox!"

He pushed trembling Veronica aside, and Etta, who has come with him, embraced her protectively, trying to calm her down, but her own heart was racing and she barely held her bearings. O'Leary meanwhile was examining the droid with a portable scanner he got from Silberstein. He hadn't managed to use the energy from scanner batteries while he was charging his accumulator, so the tool was handy now. Rasmus-Brent looked like a mechanical doll that had been switched off, with no life spark whatsoever. The only mark that something had really happened was a sooth mark on his cheek, and the other one, burnt clearly on the back of his left hand. He was clutching something in his palm.

"Yeah, that's curious..." O'Leary said finally. "Our mechanical Einstein here must have caught a saboteur in the act. He didn't stop the assailant unfortunately, but he pulled out the device the one placed in the circuit. It was hasty, because he didn't waste any time for searching the tools, he just did it with his bare hand. The whole energy impulse that was to crush the systems of passenger's compartments and the emergency air-conditioning system was shot into him."

Veronica shouted, as if she were the one who was electrocuted.

"Hush there!" O'Leary frowned. "Those women are unbearable! Most of you have less brain than a tortoise! Did I say that it cannot be fixed?"

"And can it...?"

"As soon as we have the power back. It will take a couple of hours, since I have just Leo from my old crew here, but we will have this one running!"

Veronica took a deep breath and wiped at her swollen face. As the sedative started to work and O'Leary's words were clear and re-assuring, she was slowly coming to her senses.

"I can be of use," she suggested, "I used to study cybernetics and biomechanics."

O'Leary shook his head no.

"You did, but it was a Medical Academy, not Tech. You may know everything about implants and bio-prosthetics, but it is useless knowledge when it comes to androids. It's completely different." He stood up heavily and stretched. "Woznansky, the charging of the battery is almost complete. It looks like we will be having enough energy to start the self-charging control system of the main reactor.

The chef engineer looked surprised and slightly disappointed. Etta was sure that deep inside his mind Martin Woznansky counted of O'Leary's spectacular failure and that would mean that he was right. But the thought was absurd and she pushed it away. Nobody would pray for a failure when the lives of all of them were at stake.

"So let's attend to that piece of junk you call our blessing!" the engineer murmured, as he still couldn't believe that such an analogue equipment could be of any use. He couldn't grasp the idea of assembling it in the first place. Could O'Leary foresee the catastrophe?

But Etta knew better. She remembered O'Leary's mentioning the moonshine; he wanted to have an independent power source for distilling his booze, and it came extremely useful by accident. Now it was to save them all.

"Transport Rasmus to the workshop at the engine room. But gently!" O'Leary ordered. "And nobody touches him! I'll get to work as soon as the tools are charged."

An hour later O'Leary and the chief engineer were standing at the reactor's console, looking at the flashing indicators. When the green finally turned on, meaning that the circuit was ready to self-charge, they both exhaled with relief.

"How long will it take?" O'Leary asked.

"Quite long," Woznansky answered, "since some power fluctuation can appear. We had no time to calibrate it properly, but five hours should be enough. Then the furnace will start and some thirty minutes later the power should be back. ATs should be done with welling the circuits by then. The speed those little fellas work with is really astonishing!"

"Commander Kaori deserves a promotion. She was the one who suggested using them. If we hadn't activated ATs hell knows what would be the outcome of our unfortunate situation."

"Will you also say that we all are still alive thanks to Warren's hysterical outburst?"

"Well, sort of, yes," said O'Leary in a grave voice. "Perhaps we would activate them anyway, but who knows? As you can see, even human flaws can be useful. Like my flaw of being obsessed with DIY."

Woznansky frowned, looking at the crooked, ugly battery, which was nevertheless working all right.

"So, your happy go lucky is working perfectly well. I just cannot figure out why the hell didn't you use some of manufactured batteries, if you needed-"

"I told you, I like to do it myself." O' Leary didn't feel like explaining that he needed energy for a process that would never be accepted by the captain or the supply chief, Colonel Chorvat. Of course he could lie, but one of his major flaws was being a straightforward and honest man. He'd rather have it his own way.

"All right, go back to your business, and I'm off to bed." He wrapped the conversation. "I done for tonight, and fixing Rasmus can start only after the full power is brought back.

"Will you really fix him?"

"I have no idea, to be honest... The chemo-gel will have to be replaced. And we won't know if his memory banks were damaged for quite a long time. He may turn out to be someone completely different after I'm done with fixing the mechanics. Of course, I couldn't tell that to Hornet, she is so damned attached to him!"

"I just don't understand how a real person can be switched for a robot when it comes to sex issues," murmured Woznansky.

"Don't be vulgar! Besides, Hornet treated him as a friend, no more. She has no hard time with mating with people. She used to have some sport with Nakamara, and now she has a lover here, among the crew."

"Who?"

"That's none of your business. Neither it's mine. I'm going to bed."

O'Leary yawned and dragged himself through the corridor, in the darkness, until a torch of some guard enlightened his path. The man took him to his quarters, and the doctor just fell on the bed, not even bothering with taking his shoes off.

"Is everything all right?" Derkacz asked from his upper bunk.

"Perfectly," murmured O'Leary. "Go to sleep, they can manage now without us."

The news about upcoming power regain flashed through the ship, its current lack not a danger to anyone. Relieved people moved to their rooms. They were eager to sleep through this unexpected black-out, since the temperature fell rapidly and they had some thermo insulating coverlets in their beds. Doctor Xiao sedated those who were too anxious to sleep with some pills and the craft went silent. Only one pilot, security guards and some engine room crew remained alert.

The start of the reactor began as was foreseen. The engineers watching the indicators were quite relieved when the process proceeded as planned and they could assume that the core of the reactor wasn't damaged. ATs had checked the cooling system, so they could all have some rest.

"Go to bed, Gudrun," Woznansky said. "I will stay here for a while. Kumar will replace me later. The night was rough for all of us."

"It surely was!" Silberstein yawned, taking her soiled gloves and mask off. "Night, boss!"

"Pleasant dreams. Put something cozy on before you go down, the heating will not start for a couple of hours. There are some more important systems to resuscitate."

"I know. According to my calculation the temperature will go down for some ten degrees, and the insulation shield cannot prevent that. But we will survive."

Woznansky was left alone.

The process didn't need any supervision anymore, but he wanted to check everything himself. ATs could not be completely trusted. He was alone with his opinion, but nobody protested when he scheduled the shafts so that at least one man were always present among the robots.

He sat down and rested his chin on the console, his eyes on the monitor. The green indicator was flashing reassuringly on the screen, and the rows of numbers which could be only deciphered by some of them. The reactor was about to spit energy out, all lights would go back on, and the engines would start. The contact with other shafts would be maintained. Then they would finish all the maintenance and move on. And everything would be back to normal.

For a time being.

***

The deck clock chimed four.

The door to the workshop moved, then cracked open with no sound. Somebody slipped inside, the beam of a torch sweeping the room. It stopped on the table with the motionless humanoid shape. The person moved towards the droid, put the torch away and produced something from the belt, drawing it close to the android's head. Just then was the person's arm grabbed and the emergency lights went on. The stranger's left wrist was held as well. He looked up to see the emotionless face of Raina before him. It was blank, but still her hands were clutched like steel claws.

"Well, well! Imre Kovacs!" captain Willner said. "I had expected somebody to sneak in here, but not you!"

Kovacs looked around to distinguish the captain pointing a gun at his chest.

"I just…" he stopped before he had even started.

"Yes, you, and it is so sad!" The captain turned his transmitter on. "Security, this is the captain speaking. To the workshop, now!"

The heavy steps were heard and two soldiers rushed into the room. They stopped in the door, flabbergasted.

"Arrest Kovacs!" he ordered calmly. "He is not a chief of security guards anymore. I take his degree and all the privileges. He is to be guarded day and night until I decide what to do with him, Raina, let him go, but take that object from his hand first."

Raina opened Kovac's hand with no effort and took the laser scalpel away from him. It was a precise and strong tool strong enough to open the android's skull and damage his precious memory forever.

"This is how you intend to rule? Putting machines against men?" asked Kovacs bitterly.

"You have no right to put your arguments forward. You will be judged by crew court."

"You'll be sorry, Willner!" the man shouted, as he was being dragged away.

The captain just shrugged.

"Maybe not me, but you will be sorry for sure!" he answered back and walked to the main engine room, where one of the nurses was waking engineer Woznansky.

"How is he?"

"He was blown on the head all right, a bump is quite big." The nurse answered. "We will examine him thoroughly, but it doesn't look too serious."

Silberstein, who stood nearby, was checking the reactor indicators.

"We are lucky, he didn't spoil a thing here." She sounded relieved. "He was just after the android. For now. How could you tell, captain, that he was about to come here?"

"I didn't know it was to be him, but someone." Willner put the gun away and patted his companion android on the shoulder. "Good job, Raina. Well, to be honest, Kovacs was the last suspect on my list. I wasn't sure whom I should charge for the mess, so I stayed here. Rasmus could have seen him, so the suspect was likely to come here to erase the droid's memory."

Woznansky moaned, his consciousness was coming back, but he clearly had a terrible headache. The nurse produced some painkiller.

"Inhale twice, deeply!" he instructed. "You will feel better in no time!"

"I couldn't feel any worse!"

Woznansky breathed in greedily and was soon conscious enough to worry about the reactor. He glimpsed the indicators and only then took another deep breath.

"It is all proceeding perfectly well. The lights will be back on in an hour, the heating in two and a half."

"Good, it is really chilly in here." Willner nodded. "I leave you here in your little kingdom and I'm heading back to my room. Come, my lovely, we are going to have a little rest. It has been a long night."

Next day was a mess. Everyone overslept, since the clock was deregulated and whistled the morning call in the afternoon, when everybody was wide awake and running.

The temperature and air humidity was back to normal, but still the crew was nervous and headaches were common. For the first time since they started, Stir Larson served the meal late, and cold. The kitchen utensils were "a bit broken" and there was no way to prepare anything hot. He didn't care though, the more important was that his colonies of fungi and algae, which he used to enrich lyophilized food, were not damaged.

The outer water collectors were not damaged either. They were just off and now started to work normally.

"You know, it is pretty weird to me..." Etta confided in Leonid. "Space is void, vacuum, isn't it? And we can still collect hydrogen, and quite a lot of it."

"These are only, atoms." Derkacz corrected her. "Some hundred in one square meter of it. And you can even meet whole particles. There are more of them than it was presumed earlier.

They come from comets and ice meteors. Well, they also thought earlier that the collectors like ours are impossible to construct."

"What is the working of them?"

"Hmm... how should I put it so you'd understand...? Let me give you an example: Imagine a no-gravity room, where there is a tiny cloud of iron, aluminum, copper, titanium specks dissolved around. They are so small that one cannot see them. When you turn a magnet on, only the iron specks are drawn to it. Our collectors work like that, but of course there are no magnets inside. But there is a device that works in a similar way, creating "mirror electron spin". We synthesize the hydrogen with oxygen, so steam is a product of it. And voila!"

"It still sounds too wise for me," Etta sighed.

They were seated in the conference room, waiting for the captain and the remaining crew members to arrive. It was an emergency situation and nobody was really surprised that they were all called in.

Engineer Woznansky, doctor Xiao, Veronica Hornet and Camus de Bernal arrived.

"Where is O'Leary?" asked Willner, who came the last and was eyeing the small crowd.

"He is getting the equipment ready to fix Rasmus," Veronica answered.

"Well, then, to cut the long story short, report, de Bernal." The captain waved his hand.

The chief pilot coughed.

"The communication is back. The remaining crafts, seeing us stop, turned back and circled us, waiting for the proceedings. The commanders had some video conference and decided that if none activity appeared for six hours, they were to proceed according to emergency rescue procedures. We are lucky they didn't do that, because the outcome may be devastating. Next point: the re-start of the engines and the steering panel is successful. We are now trying to re-gain our initial acceleration. And that would be all for now."

"Doctor Xiao?"

"No one was harmed if we don't count their shattered nerves. Due to the temperature fluctuation some minor infections of throat may occur, but we can easily cure that. The biological department wasn't seriously damaged. The crops survived, but some of them may cease to grow for some time."

"Derkacz, what about your issues?"

"All equipment is back to work. All the damage repaired. That's it."

"Miss Hornet?"

"The morale is quite high, but..." Veronica hesitated. "Once Kovacs is in jail, who is going to be the chief of security guards?"

"I have thought of that," The captain pushed a call button on his console.

The door slid open and a tall, massive man, labeled as major, appeared in the frame. He had a nice face and smiling eyes, indicating honesty. It was not a misguiding impression: major La Ver was well known for his righteousness and openness; he was also completely devoted to his service.

"La Ver, I officially nominee you as a chief of security on the mother ship," The captain addressed him. "You will claim Kovac's quarters, who was dismissed for a treason. Lieutenant

Colonel Borden, the leader of the troops, agreed to your nomination."

"Oh, my, I mean, yes, Sir!" La Ver saluted, but his round face was still surprised.

Etta noticed sheer satisfaction in her friend's gaze. She had suspected that Veronica and this bear-like giant soldier are pretty close, but she didn't dare to ask. She sometimes didn't approve of her friends love hunts, but she had never said a word of scold. This time Etta felt the choice was right. Sherman La Ver, the master of arms and war tactics was the best pick in the crew. Apart from his size and a nature of his profession, he was a mild man, but he was capable of keeping order among his soldiers. That nomination was a good call.

***

After the meeting Veronica rushed to the engine room. Etta followed, but even though she was interested in Rasmus condition, but she knew a lot more about the functioning of droids, and it meant that her hopes for bringing that one back were futile. The electric shock must have burned data banks, and the new synapses wouldn't function as effectively as the old ones. The personality of Rasmus might have changed completely.

"Brent. Veronica wants him to be named Brent." Etta thought.

Derkacz passed her.

"Do not go there," he insisted. "MacLean hates it when anyone observes him at work. We will inform you as soon as we finish."

Veronica stopped, sad and brooding. She had that look on her face, as if she were a sister and somebody forbade her to accompany her brother in rough moments of his life.

"I thought I would wait..."

"What for? It will take a couple of hours. Do something useful instead of staying here." Derkacz stopped, frowning his bushy brows. "I mean it, girls. The engine room is not a place for you." He stepped into the room and closed the door behind him.

"Girls!" Veronica sneered. "Girls, mind you! The old fart!"

"He's not that old, is he?" Etta threw her friend a questioning look and then glanced back at the closed door.

"Oh yes, he is. He's nearly sixty. He doesn't look so, but I saw his files and I know the year of his graduation."

Etta took her arm and dragged her down the corridor.

"Come to my room. We'll play some cards with Raoul and relax. We are of no use here, and Kumar is making faces at us already."

It was a common knowledge that the engine room staff didn't like any intruders in their area. It was excused, though: only the specialized crew knew the fragile equipment, and the lives of everyone depended on it. They cherished the placed, kept it sparkling clean, but the heat inside was unbearable!

Etta stopped.

She suddenly visualized a deserted, scorched place filled with deformed human skeletons, covered in rags, hideous and monstrous, looking for anything they could devour. Those pictured she had known from the pictures, it was Europe right after the First Catastrophe, that was inflicted by people. No, not by people, by governments that were sick with greed and pride, wanting more and more to rule upon. One attack after another, until there was nothing and no one to rule upon. The Old World that used to be beautiful turned into a moon-like desert, even the air poisonous. Whoever was too weak or slow to run from the contamination, this one was dying. Many refugees also died from radiation. Why was she there?

"Etta, what's wrong?" Veronica's voice reached her as if from a great distance.

Remember what they had taught you. Don't let those pictures cloud your mind. Not everything you see and hear is real. But the scorched ground, smoldering ruins, those clumsy, deformed bodies and the sky, that low-hanging, blood-red sky... And the dust, whirling, and whirling...

"Get me out of here, quick!" Etta whispered before she fainted, sliding to the ground.

She couldn't hear her friend screaming.

VIII

Etta was the first who got hit by the strange disease. Many followed: the engine room technicians, two soldiers, Callum, Doctor O'Leary and two of three pilots. The symptoms were always the same: fever, hallucinations, collapsing. It was considered a sabotage at first, then virus, finally a bacterial infection. None of the tests resulted in finding microbes, though. After a long search doctor Xiao recognized the fungus that was fit for a cause. It was a rare, artificially bred species, which must have been taken on board by accident.

"How could that happen?" The captain was worried. "What do we do now? We cannot use the fungicide, it would destroy all our colonies, and we cannot breathe that in!"

"Let's face it, we cannot get rid of it," the doctor said in a flat voice. "We can only lower the air humidity, and that would keep it away. I will compose a vaccination that would prevent the rest of the crew and the settlers from getting infected after they wake up."

"Why only some of us got sick?"

"Well, it seems that the fungus attacked those who had a respiratory infection in the past. Miss Solis was the first one who got sick, because she had a viral throat infection lately. It is the same mechanism that worked during the plagues. The first ones to die were those who had suffered pneumonia in the past. It is good that this fungus isn't a fast-spreading one. It was artificially developed and is used to make psychotropic medicine. When it is not contaminated it causes visions like those one could get after eating "the mushrooms", you know, the wild ones. And here it causes fever, disorientation and respiratory problems, but fortunately all those are easy to cure. I have isolated the sick, and Raul turns out to be a perfect nurse for them. And he is easier to de-contaminate, since UV rays don't do him any harm."

Doctor Xiao yawned. She hadn't slept in three days and her body sustained with invigorants needed a rest. Captain Willner smiled.

"I thought you didn't like the droids," he said crossly.

The doctor shrugged.

"Why would I care about them? Do I like a clamp of a blood pressure measure? I accept their existence. We shouldn't threat them as if they were humans, and they should know their place in a row. If we stick to that, everything is going to be in order. Speaking of order, do you know what happens with Rasmus? We could use him now."

"O'Leary says that re-activation was successful. Talk to Veronica about the details."

"I'd rather not. She doesn't like me, you know."

"Just don't talk bad about the droid in her presence, it should keep her civil."

Xiao just nodded wearily. He slant eyes were narrowed and circled in black, her elfish face gray and sunken. She was hard to like, her temper was short and remarks sarcastic, but she put all she had into her work. And she didn't care for her condition.

"Go to bed, now!" Willner said in a stone-hard voice. "Your time can cope with everything, and you can always be woken up if they don't. You are dismissed, private Xiao!"

Even though she was exhausted, she managed to smile.

"One more thing before I follow your order, sir. I have some important information for you and it cannot wait."

"What is it?"

"When the epidemic began, I tested the blood of all the crew members, even the prisoner. His blood type doesn't match with the one in his personal file. You know, it comes first in the results print. I double checked it. The sample is in a DNA sequencer now. You will be informed as soon as we get the results."

Kirk Willner whistled through his teeth.

"And now you are talking! It would be a great relief if the prisoner was a fraud. I know Imre Kovacs since we were but brats, his treason was like a rock upon my chest. And now, be a good girl and off you go to your bed, before I need to slap you!"

"Aye, sir!" Xiao saluted in a funny way and rushed away, leaving the captain with his thoughts.

Meanwhile Etta was lying on the bed in a makeshift hospital. She was sipping a cocktail of proteins, energizers, medicines and vitamins; her back was supported comfortably. She couldn't digest solids yet, but she was too weak to feel hungry anyway.

"I could have died, you know," she said to Raul between the sips. She sounded surprised, as if she has just realized how fragile her body was, how frail her life.

"No, you couldn't," Raul answered mildly. "Your body would have fought the infection even without medicine. You are far stronger than you realize.

Perhaps it was as he has said. Droids never lied. Well, only after they had been clearly instructed to do so.

"I saw a nuclear wasteland before I collapsed." Etta Shrugged. "It was the landscape I had digitally produced with Jim Mildred while we were in college. Why did I see that horrible stuff?"

"It was so because you remember it so well, from your classes, and from various presentations. It was so because you think about it too much, you think too much about what happened before we rose from the ashes." It was O'Leary talking from his bed. "Not many of us know as much about those days as you do. Are you aware what are all those students' projections used for?"

"Are they used for anything?"

"Of course they are! They are propaganda tools used against the rebels. They are used to show the opponents of our laws to what monstrosities can freedom lead to. Freedom of a rich individual. A person fed with the pictures of the world shredded by "The Mistake War" for days, the person fed with pictures of natural selection and the documentaries of chaos and terror that the war had produced, walks out of the re-socialization center happy with the idea that there is food and air around and available."

O'Leary crossed his long arms under his head.

He had noticed some time ago that the young teacher left some historical issues unsaid. He had known the history all too well, and was tempted many a time to add the drastic details that she had mercifully covered in silence.

"Is that true that the western hemisphere hadn't been destroyed by that was because wiser people had lived there?" asked Raul suddenly.

All heads turned in his direction, surprised by his peculiar interest.

O'Leary laughed ironically.

"That's absurd! It was pure luck. And the aftershock of what had happened cleared peoples' minds a little. And our western hemisphere had also been affected. Radioactive pollution, animals and plants dying on a mass scale, we've been through all that. And it resulted in chaos."

And it was chaos, indeed. No food, no medicine, no fresh water. The wave of immigrants that had to be taken care of. Most of them died anyway, but some thrived, especially those who escaped radioactive pollution. They settled on the Latin grounds, as they were named in those days. They were welcomed, or unwanted. And they were all to survive the decades of struggle to survive and suffering the military terror. Etta has almost felt guilty when she looked back from her cozy perspective. Her generation lacked nothing. She had her points limited, but she was the one to decide what to buy for her points, while her parents were struggling to survive on the ratios. They were given a sheet of plastic with ratios printed on it: protein concentrate, starch, fiber, and saccharine, fresh water. And nothing more. If you used it too fast, you were starving till the beginning of next month.

The situation improved after the resources on the dark side of the moon were discovered. Something was there, and Etta didn't even know what it was, but it increased the production of food back on earth. It must have been some fertilizing mineral, as many of that kind were discovered on the moon.

"Tell me something, Mac," Etta asked, putting the empty cup on the table. "How was the modern engine discovered? Our cruise wouldn't be possible without it. Neither would space stations and bases on various planets built. Even moon mining wouldn't work without it. How could our ancestors have missed it?"

O'Leary fixed his position in the bed.

"Because they have missed some significant details, my dear. It is not the fuel that matters, but the engine. "The absolute factory" reactor."

"What?"

"Karel Capek novel, the "R.U.R." dude. He had some really interesting books written. One of them was a treaty about the motor that could fully use the energy it produced. It was science-fiction in his are, but there were people in the days of fuel crisis that have finally built the prototype. Of course, it hadn't used one hundred percent of the energy, but ninety six, but it was more than enough."

"They have constructed it and...?"

"It started and exploded. And the only remnant of fuel in the crater it produced was the coal nugget of a size of a walnut. One of the constructors died on the spot, the other had fought for his life for two months. But they had proven the impossible. When the time came to modify and perfect the engine, the firs self-sustaining link was produced."

"My heart..." Raul whispered, placing the hand on his chest.

O'Leary frowned.

"You shouldn't know those things! The andropology should be kept away from you, so you couldn't built your replicas."

"Yes, sir, I am aware of that."

The exchange remained Etta about the important matter.

"Raul, how is Brent doing? Have you talked to Veronica?"

"Rasmus is getting better. He has some difficulties with verbal communication, but he has already regained his speech. There are some white spots in his memory. But he is fine otherwise, and Derkacz says that he will fix those minor disabilities."

"Veronica must be so happy! I cannot imagine her losing him!"

"Signum temporis," O'Leary sighed. He scratched his side under the pajamas and sat straight.

"Why did you say that?" asked one of the patients, and the Irishman shot his a cold gaze.

"Because it is so, Chiavez. Some sort of people, and I mean introvert, zero-type, can only have the company of androids, so they treat them as if they were real people, their family. A human being must have something to love. And it is kind of weird when we consider Miss Hornet, who cannot whine about lacking male company. Well, perhaps a friend is more difficult to find than a lover."

"You should know the feeling," murmured Chiavez.

"No, I don't."

"You don't? How come?" The technician and other patients looked at the doctor flabbergasted.

Only Etta seemed vaguely surprised. She has suspected for a while that he wasn't a zero, He used to have a wife. The rest of the crew though were sure that the doctor's rough personality was a result of his zero category.

"I'm a three," said O'Leary bitterly.

"No way!"

"What are you doing here?"

"Why haven't you got a regular family?"

The questions bombed him from everywhere. Even corporeal Svensen, still pretty weak, lifted herself on elbows to better hear. O'Leary sneered, half-amused, half-pitiful.

"I like to think of my own!" he said, crawling out of bed. "I can breed, but it doesn't mean I have to do it. I'm not a rabbit. Sorry, boys and girls, it was a nice chat, but I am called by my unavoidable duties!"

After uttering this pompous statements he want to one of the toilets. The patients started to discuss the news immediately, and even Svensen, though nauseated, tried to participate. That was out of everybody's minds: somebody who is allowed to have kids not wanting them?

Etta was out of it. She was deep in her thoughts, looking at the ceiling. She was a historian, knowing all the mechanisms that led to forming that way of thinking. Being allowed to breed was not only a matter of genes. A variety of other characteristics were being taken into consideration: health, emotional stability, education, job or lack of it, police files, and so forth. All crimes against legal breeding were severely punished. The babies that were illegally born were taken from their parents and given to selected foster families. They were also taken from criminals, toxic substances addicts, mentally ill and unstable. If the baby was born disabled in any way, the parents were automatically crossed out of further breeding program. Veronica's parents were granted a permission for one more child after she'd been born with split palate. The condition was caused by a minor stir in chromosome line, otherwise she was perfectly healthy. And her brother, Burton, was born strong and healthy.

Some time ago it took brutal terror to indoctrinate people into conscious breeding. Nowadays they were all sure of its righteousness, because they were taught since early years that it was all for common good. The army and police helped to create job posts for scientists and constructors, and those were the ones who invented and built the safe and sterile world. The basic rule of it was "Stick to the law and you will not get into trouble." And trouble meant as bad as going to jail and staying there permanently. It was impossible to run, it was impossible to hide, so people quickly learned to stay straight to the rules. The only remnant of the Dark Times was the irrational, subconscious revulsion of those wearing uniforms.

So how were people chosen for breeding? Etta decided to ask captain when she would have a chance, she couldn't remain ignorant in that matter. Or maybe major LaVer was a better option to ask? He was becoming talkative whenever Veronica was around, and that he had a crush on her was all too visible, he just couldn't hide it. Yep, they were more than one topic to talk about. But for now Etta had closed her eyes and fell deep into long, invigorating sleep.

***

Raul swiped the hair back from his Domina's face and put a blanket over her body. Making sure that she was fast asleep he walked to corporal Svensen's bed and gave her the medicine doctor Xiao had prescribed. No one else needed his assistance. The crisis was fading, people were getting better and the quarantine was about to be over soon. Pilots were the ones who wanted to be back to service as soon as possible. Mitsuo Quang was getting along perfectly well without the remaining members of the crew, because the human factor was just the assistance for auto-pilot. But the humans were a crisis option. They could pilot the ship, but lack the machine's precision and speed of reactions. They were the only hope for the ship nevertheless if the machines would fail.

***

Doctor Celine Xiao was not chosen for a head doctor of the flag ship because she was the daughter of the famous professor Xiao. Her own work was good enough to nominate her. Colonel Gongadze had to admit that nobody else would be skillful enough to isolate and determine the illness-causing factor. And she also prepared the vaccination for the rest of the crew.

"We should have expected that," sighed the colonel. "The fungi are extremely vicious and immune, there is no way to exterminate them."

"That is why I have decided to go for a vaccination, not for a fungicide," Xiao answered. "Of course we will pour some antiseptic over literally everything, but we won't fight it all, for sure. My vaccination will make the crew immune to the toxin from the mold. And we have to give to everyone, for if the toxin is here, it is on all the ships, but lays dormant."

"And why is that so?"

"I think it was woken by the changes in the environment after the systems breakdown. The air dried due to the humidifiers being gone, but the circulation was running. The temperature lowered. And when all the systems started to run again, the humidity and temperature rose, triggering the waking of the toxin."

Gongadze shook his head. He used to have a mane of hair and a moustache, looking like a dictator from olden days in the picture hanging on the wall of the War Museum. Only the pipe in his teeth was missing. Doctor Xiao couldn't remember the man's name. He was one in the Ancient Monsters gallery.

"You did well, Xiao," Gongadze said, "and due to your fast action we could give the medicine to those infected and start the sterilization process. Spraying the fungicide would be more effective, but it would ruin our yeasts crops. We cannot afford to lose it."

"That's true," she acclaimed. "We need it."

After a moment of silence Gongadze sighed and asked:

"And what about our prisoner?"

"Nothing new. We still don't know his identity, but he is not Kovacs for sure. He won't talk, and he has an implant somewhere that neutralizes the truth serum. I just cannot identify where it had been sewn in. The captain reported everything we know to the ground control. They are about to report back if they know anything."

"Even if they knew, what would it change now?" murmured the colonel. "What is the old man planning to do with that cuckoo's egg?"

The doctor shrugged. They couldn't send him back; the only solutions was to keep him locked or terminate him. Nobody was prone to do either.

"Let's vaccinate the rest of the crew," she said, sighing. "I need to visit the remaining ships. Jimenez insisted I do it as soon as possible."

"So go follow your orders."

The actual cruising from one ship to another was able in the space ferries, but only the pilots were allowed to drive them. Many soldiers had finished some flying courses, but without official papers they were not allowed to pilot anything. It was not a blank formality, but a necessity. The passenger's cabins had no windows, because the sight of the star-specked vacuum around the ships could result in some nervous breakdown in case of people who were not thoroughly trained to handle that vast idea of infinity. And a person who broke down sitting at the steering console could produce only havoc and permanent damage to the priceless equipment. And that was why The Space Agency introduced all of the restrictions. Only the strongest and mentally stable people were chosen for pilots; they were thoroughly trained not only at steering, but also at detecting and maintaining minor equipment damage. And those people were valued in every space cruise, even the short one.

Doctor Xiao was taken to all of the ships to apply her vaccination, making the crew sterilize their ships at the same time. The mother ship was the only one where the sickness at the developed stadium was noted. Aisha Bahrani was another person who got sick, and the pathogens were there only in the blood of few star sailors.

"It could have been worse," said Kenneth Linde during the video conference of all the doctors. We are managing quite well. The antidepressants work, the crew got used to the environment and the hardships of the flight, and we do not expect any pregnancies, do we?

"That was quite a poor joke," Lisbeth Mell from Viking 04 sneered." I have checked the files and we have three fertile women in our lines. What will you say to that, doctor Gongadze?"

"And who would that be?"

"Sookie Hashimato, Perla Jones and Gudrun Silberstein. They are all classified as ones."

"Let's check if they take proper contraceptives. Maybe it was only Linde's joke, but the pregnancy on board would be extremely uncomfortable."

"It would be impossible to accept," underlined Celine Xiao. "The gravity fluctuates, no sunlight, no milk. Besides, only Silberstein is the one we have to worry about."

"And why is that so?"

"Hashimato and Jones are lovers, so there won't be any pregnancy here. Well, unless one of them changes her mind. None of them will be granted a conception license according to the law."

"And I was beginning to wonder what the ones are doing here!" Linde laughed lewdly. "Let me remind you that there is no Demography Department here, so law may malfunction."

"Don't you accuse anyone without a clear evidence!" Tengiz Gongadze frowned. "Hashimato and Jones are my crew and are under my protection. Both are honest and reasonable. None of them would think about any foolishness. But Silberstein is another issue and we need to talk to her about it."

"I have already done that," said Xiao crossly. "She advised me to keep my nose in my medical business and stay out of the engine room."

The doctors burst with laughter at that remark. All the engineers were well known for their slapping mouths, but nobody expected Silberstein o be alike. She used to be quiet and calm, out of everybody's way, all up into her engines and diagnostic computers.

"There is nothing to laugh about!" Xiao barked. "That is a serious issue! The only good thing for now is that the woman isn't in any relationship now. Well, let's hope that she isn't, and if so, that she is being precautious."

When O'Leary heard the after talk of that exchange, he laughed out loud stating that nobody managed to prevent a horny woman from an affair in the whole history of mankind. He scolded the doctors for worrying about a hypothetical pregnancy and not minding their running business. And he was quite right, as not everything was proceeding as planned. The fungus fever was tamed, but some new symptoms occurred among the people at all of the ships. They suffered gums bleeding, severe pain and problems with uttering the speech. Blood tests didn't show any pathogens, and no fever or mood fluctuations followed. Almost all of the crew had trouble with chewing and when paradonthosis was detected, colonel Gongadze woke up.

"We should all be shameful for not figuring this out! We are not on earth anymore! These are the results of gravity fluctuations and eating mash! Cannot it be tuned up a little?"

"No," said Bahrani with all the conviction. "Gravity generators work in waves, because the magnetic field fluctuates. And only that fluctuations causes their generating of the gravity. If we cancel the pulse, the field would be gone. It needs to oscillate between zero points seven and zero point nine gram. And we should all be glad that the differences are so slight. It was said not so long ago that to keep the gravity we need zero point five amplitude. And the flight would look like a sea cruise then, with everyone suffering from headaches and vomiting. And, compared to the gravity at the decks of-"

"Spare us the detailed lecture!" Gongadze stopped her. "It is enough that we cannot cut the cause of our problems, we can only cure the symptoms."

"How can we cure the symptoms?" the captain asked.

"We will prescribe some calcium, and the food technicians would have to make us some resilient chewing gum. The crew must provide some work out for the teeth and gums, otherwise we will reach out destination toothless. If we reach it at all."

Captain Willner frowned.

"You could have bitten your tongue, colonel!"

"Sorry, captain. I have those doubts from time to time. Some of the crew at Viking 05 tried to get off the ship; there was a suicide of an engineer at Viking 02, and we would all be victims without those mental stabilizers."

"What do you mean "get off the ship"?" asked Veronica, who was there as a coordinator.

"Just like that, open the gate and get off, but where to, no one knew. They are stable now, after some sedalithiol infusion, but there is no guarantee that episodes like that won't occur anymore."

"We can guarantee nothing. And we are responsible for everything," said Willner in a dry voice. "Just take a good care of the crew health, doctors. We have a lot of spare parts for the machines, but we cannot replace people. We have already lost a few, and one is locked in the prison and is staying there, as long as I am the commander of this flight."

That nameless prisoner was a pin in the ass. Although the real Imre Kovacs was alive, it was impossible to discover who that man here was. He was in a bad shape and must have been treated roughly in the past.

"That could have been Tesla annihilator," informed colonel Tomasi from the headquarters. "The man cannot recall a thing."

It was an extreme controversial psychiatric tool. The heavy magnetic field could erase the patient memory completely, leaving him or her oblivious and at the re-socializing crew mercy. The patient learned to be a completely different person under their custody. The tool was designed to erase the minds of the heaviest criminals, but the project could not be forced through the human rights lawyers' wall. The possibility of the extremist putting their hands on such a dangerous tool made the government and generals quiver.

What could they do with Kovac's doppelganger? He would be executed on Earth by now, that was more than sure. But people on a spaceship, so far away from their planet, changed their point of view. Every human being was irreplaceable. And Kirk Willner just couldn't condemn him to death. So the prisoner stayed locked in his room, with armed guards at his door. The crew was split into two camps: some wanted him dead, the others said that keeping him locked in such a small space was nothing else than torture. The only one who was silent was Veronica. Hating the man silently for trying to destroy Rasmus, she didn't intend to speak. She knew that her judgment was not objective at all.

"We need to decide finally," O'Leary said when somebody asked his opinion. "Otherwise out Malcolm X will go mad due to his claustrophobic situation and then we would have a serious problem."

But until nobody came with the idea that would be safe for both the crew and the prisoner, the last one remained locked.

IX

For four days major LaVer had been drilling the crew so they would be prepared for "a collision with minor flying object", so everyone were more than annoyed when the siren woke them up in the middle of the night again.

"And why would it be a minor object?" asked Ian Callum, mad that he was being dragged away from his work again.

"Because if it were major, you wouldn't even have time to pray," LaVer explained, undisturbed.

The four night long drill drudged all of the crews simultaneously. Bu it was essential to check if they still remembered all they had been taught back on Earth. Could they really co-operate in case of emergency?

The chiefs of security were to analyze the results. And they just couldn't do it now, because this time the emergency was real. Before the people were woken up enough to curse and look for the one responsible for a wakeup call, the siren roared again, this time accompanied by the metallic voice: *Attention all decks! Human life hazard!*

It meant that all of the hands should be ready to help and all the ships would come to an immediate halt. And something really bad must have happened, because the procedure hadn't been used even in case of false Kovacs sabotage.

It took but a minute for all of them, human and android alike, to stand at their spots, fully equipped and uniformed. Of course, some minor problems like illness and that unfortunate sabotage occurred, but nothing as serious as to stop the whole convoy. They used to laugh at the possibility of alien attack, which would cause to use the most serious emergency procedures, and now some of the crew members whose imagination started to work suggested the possibility.

"Nonsense!" Leonard Derkacz's voice was weary. "Even if some prodigy unearthly geniuses came up with the idea of visiting our space backyard, why the hell would they use the same course? And what would they look for in this middle of nowhere? We are not on some space highway! The space is big enough to avoid the collision! And the probability of-

"With all due respect, doctor, but you are lacking any imagination!" Larson, the technician, seemed disappointed by the man's lack of enthusiasm in the matter of the encounter.

Derkacz looked down at him.

"And you are being imaginative?" he asked. "That's not any imagination, that's ignorance! You are the cook, so you can come up with such ridiculous ideas, but why is engineer Bahrani saying the same, I cannot tell! I really expected that woman to be more reasonable!"

"That man is not only looking like the droid, he is behaving like one!" Larson whispered to corporal Svensen, who seemed to agree.

She was not the only one to thing Derkacz was the weirdest person on board. He was worse even than O'Leary, but didn't care what other thought. And the rumor said that not even the artificial woman managed to stay at his side. That was not true, of course. He just lost interest in Reina, and that was why she was the Captain's companion now. They shared some peculiar friendship, the droid knew how Derkacz had helped her and saw in him a kind of father figure. And Leonid, harboring many warm feelings for her, earned the nick name of "the old man's in-law".

"Can we tell what exactly happened?" asked MacLean O'Leary when the captain finally appeared.

"Oh, yes, we can," Kirk Willner was dark as a storm cloud. "While we were playing with the imagined emergency, one of the technician, John Warens, stole one of the capsules that contained Leila Sabatini, put it into the ferry and launched towards *Enceladus*. He is likely to ask for some kind of asylum there."

"Is he mad?" Ian Callum cried. "Enceladus Prime is a scientific colony, not some foreign country!"

Willner shrugged, not knowing what John Warens could think while planning his escape. "And why did he chose Leila Sabatini in particular?" he asked commander Kaori whose face just appeared on the screen. The chief of Viking 03 looked disturbed, but not shattered.

"I don't know, but the problem is more complex that we might have assumed," she reported. "I checked Warens files and it turned out that he wasn't granted the pilot's license due to his weak psyche. He has all the skills, though. The other thing is that that it was the double capsule. It contains the mother and her six month old child, the boy named David."

"Were they in a relationship?"

"We cannot confirm that. What we know though is Warrens' opinion on the existence of Jewel system. He didn't believe that it was even real, both the system and the planet, Patris. He claimed we would have to turn back to Enceladus anyway, and the long journey was a hazard for everyone."

"I have a bad feelings about this."

"Me to. If Warens brakes the capsule both the mother and the baby are likely to die."

"When did it happen?"

"Thirty two hours ago. He has enough oxygen and supplies to run for a week."

The captain pressed the intercom button.

"To the bridge. Calculate the time of getting to Enceladus at a maximum safe speed. And the chase trajectory," he commanded.

All went silent. Chasing the ferry meant breaking the ultimate rule, and that was changing the convoy's course. They didn't know the captain's intentions, but they trusted in him. He was the leader and he had to find the solution. It was the only way.

If captain Willner doubted his ways in that moment, nobody could know that. He stood motionless, waiting for the pilots to response, with his arms crossed at his broad chest and his face as blank as Reina's, who accompanied him. After a few long minutes the buzz of incoming call sounded in silence.

"The route is calculated, sir." Jimenez reported. "According to the signals Warens doubled the critical numbers, but he won't get to the station. The only thing we can do is to chase him with a quadruple safe speed in another ferry. We called him via voice and signals. The ferry is silent."

O'Leary whistled, others just exchanged glances. It meant one of the ships would have to alter its course. Otherwise the ferry and its passengers were doomed.

"It is logical that he is silent. He stole the ferry and some hibernated passengers, did you really expect he would answer our first call?"

"I will go," said major LaVer. "I am experienced at critical speed flying."

"Nonsense!" burst doctor Xiao. "It is not a moment in deceleration capsule, we are talking hours of flight! Your respiratory system would fail! I do not agree to that!"

"No human can survive such speed," said engineer Woznansky with authority.

"Human, no," Willner confirmed and all of his companions understood what he meant.

"Rasmus is a good pilot," it was O'Leary who spoke. "He was through variety of training. He is fixed. And he can go."

Veronica turned pale, the tears welling in her eyes, but she managed to remain silent. Etta grasped her hand. She was also deeply moved, even though she knew there was no other way. The droids couldn't be affected by lack of oxygen or critical speed, they reacted faster than humans and what were most important - they didn't get panic attacks.

The captain switched to conference mode.

"Attention all decks! We are sending a rescue ferry for the refugees. Prepare the crew: Ruslana 39F, Roger 7E, Roy 98D. Rasmus 101A will pilot the ferry. Raul 209C will oversee the Mission. Officer Denberry, make sure that the ferry is ready to go. Report readiness to launch in ten minutes."

"Yes, sir!"

Etta felt her fingers grow cold. She looked at Veronica; her friend seemed to mumble something under her breath, her eyes in the ground.

"What are you saying?"

"I'm saying that I have just realized something," Veronica looked at Etta.

"What is it?"

"Is Denberry human?"

"Of course he is, why do you think otherwise?"

"His name is Rod."

Etta sighed. It was not a good moment to munch on that!

"His name is Elrod, they just call him Rod since he was a kid. He was through facial nerves paralysis when he was at school, and you know how cruel could children be. He had no mimics at all, his face was like a mask. The brats nicknamed him the droid, Rod, instead of Danny, as they used to call him before the stroke."

Veronica just turned round and run from the room, so nobody could see her tears.

Etta followed. She felt numb realizing the rescue Mission could fail, but she kept her composure. She was already through the possible loss of her android companion. Nevertheless she could see that Veronica was more emotional than ever. She wanted to soothe her friend's nerves, but when she approached Veronica's room, Sherman LaVer was already inside and was cuddling Veronica to his broad chest, whispering some comforting words into her ear. Etta recoiled.

Love is a strange but nice thing...

LaVer was really in love in Veronica, and even though she used to be extremely picky, whatever that meant, now she seemed to be also fond of the officer. They weren't a perfect match, not at all, but it could work.

The long flight produced a lot of unusual matches. Those relationships were formed not only for satisfying the sexual need. People had many other needs, needs of interaction with each other in many simple deeds: talking, reading, holding hands while sharing their hopes and fears, even quarreling. And they all fear for one another. Even O'Leary formed some kind of bond with doctor Xiao, and the seemingly heartless Derkacz spend a lot of time around Elsa Silberstein. Was Etta and the captain the only ones who didn't find a match on board? But the captain couldn't just play Casanova on his ship. He had to keep his distance. Besides, he had Reina who stood up to his needs, who looked up to him and was practically his shadow. He could not ignore that: there was this deep conviction in her mind that she was only alive because her Dominants allowed her to live. Dario at first, then Leonid Derkach, and now the captain. She thought it was perfectly all right that her owner could whatever he wished with her. No conversations with Derkacz could undo that. But no one could foresee her reaction if the captain were to form a relationship with a real woman.

And Etta, who was a shy introvert, wasn't eager to look for male companionship on board. She dated a man once or twice, and it was more than enough for her. She was satisfied with Raul and befriending her anthropology teacher, O'Leary. Even though they got along pretty well, their friendship had no erotic tinge to it. Etta felt from time to time that she could fell for the captain, but she subdued the feeling. Even if she really liked him, it would be more than inappropriate to show it to a commander.

Etta moved to the ferry land spot, where the captain was already talking to Rasmus. He was instructing the droid, trying to be as precise as he could. What was surprising, the captain called the droid "Brent", as if he acknowledged his right to having a human name. Could Raul have a real, human name? Which one would suit him? Clark? Or Lorenzo?

But Raul was Raul. That was his name. End of the matter.

As if calling him with her thought, Etta's companion appeared in the landing. He was wearing his uniform, some extra tool belt and a first aid kit hung from his shoulder.

"I thought it could be useful," he said. "Warens may need some medical assistance.

"Good guess. Have you got some pacifier inside?"

Raul produced a distance injector, a tiny air gun that could shoot the medicine Missile at a long distance. The minute capsule pointed with a needle would inject the sedative right into the patient's system when it hit the target.

"Doctor Xiao has given the sedater to me. It will put the engineer down in a second.

"Good. But please, try to avoid any unnecessary violence. Maybe Warens can be reasoned with." The captain's voice was more of a request than an order.

Etta shrugged. The needles weren't used anymore, and right after the ecological apocalypse they were used only to drawing blood and vaccination. Modern injectors worked perfectly well without them, and the feeling one got when the medicine got under the skin was nothing in comparison with old-fashioned needle stab. No wonder some people collapsed when facing them.

"Don't worry, captain. We will do our best not to bring humans any harm.

The captain smiled at Etta.

"This is a matter of no precedence. The rescue team of androids collaborating in space. We need to trust our Companions in this one, since we cannot send people."

"They won't fail. I am sure of that!"

"Me too, but it is a virgin Mission, so I feel a little... tense."

But the captain looked more than a little tense. He was pale, his forehead and temples beaded with sweat. One could see he could barely remain calm. The law on Earth was clear: no situation could put a man's life only on the android's concern. And the captain had no other choice. He chose only the robots he trusted completely. Some of them were fairly unpredictable, because they were not programmed to obey, as robots were. If the order stood in contrast with the android's way of thinking, the machine could decline. Independent thinking meant the will to choose. The opponents of 'andropologization' of the society held it as their main flag. *We do not know what they are thinking. Won't they go riot without following our orders?* Those shouting rights like that seemed to forget that the androids would have to find a reasonable cause for rioting. The artificial humans were being ostracized against the facts and without any reason. And the anti-droid lobby was so strong that the androids weren't even close to becoming a part of rescue team, even if they could be more efficient than humans. And here it was: the rescue team of android that were to save three humans, without any human supervise. Kirk Willner was sure that no one would tolerate any of it on Earth.

Attention, the ferry approaching the ship!

The metallic voice of the cruise control filled the landing hall.

"Proceed with the landing!" said the captain into the wall microphone.

Confirmed. Please stand back from the safety line.

Everyone stepped back instinctively, even though they were at a safe distance from the dock.

The clear panel slid up, dividing the oxygenated room from the dock that was about to open.

Decompression.

The air pumps hissed, and the docked cracked opened. The ferry marked Viking 04 slid inside and landed in one of the empty spots, the magnetic clasps holding him firmly. The wall closed behind it.

Oxygenation.

The air pumps hissed again and after a while the panel slid down. They could approach the ferry safely.

The door of the raft opened. The captain looked at Raul and Rasmus.

"Go, then," he said. "We have no time to waste, so I won't be giving you any speech. Good luck!"

Etta wanted to say something but bit her tongue. She was glad that major LaVer managed to keep Veronica away, convinced her to stay put at her quarters. She wouldn't stand this good bye. Etta couldn't understand why Veronica was being so emotional when it came to Rasmus, or Brent. Veronica had many real men around, hadn't she? Resolute, pretty, graceful and easygoing, she had many friends, both male and female. She seemed to be the last in need of a Companion. And she wasn't really. Rasmus was assigned to her as a kind of intern at her scientific projects. And she became somewhat addicted to him, he became essential, even though he wasn't a real Companion but more of an assistant.

And he was heading to the ferry now, welcomed by one of the Viking 04 pilots, Vito Carver.

"All systems working. I have checked the reserve oxygen bottles for your human passenger," he said to the android.

"I am sure you did, officer. I'm taking the steering from here on."

The pilot took the wrist decoding panel and handed it to Rasmus. The ferry couldn't start without it, co the pilots kept them close. No one could guess how Warens came to have one of those. The investigation was postponed till the refugees were safely brought back.

Raul and Rasmus boarded the ferry. The door closed, the hermetic wall rose again and the metallic voice pronounced the warnings with no emotion. In a moment the ferry was out there, in the void. And the team of androids had no one to supervise them.

The captain let no one to hang around the launching post. Everyone was to go to the chores, and if somebody had nothing to do, double checking the job already done would also do the trick. Willner was willing to tell any news by himself. He took his post alone, on the bridge.

Etta tried to make some notes in her chronicle, but she couldn't stop thinking about the captain. She had known him well enough to know that he wouldn't sleep or eat until he got some message from the ferry. She also felt it was going to be a sleepless night.

The slight knock on the door startled her.

"Enter!" she cried, ready to welcome Veronica or doctor O'Leary, but discovering to her surprise Reina at her doorstep. The android was just standing there, as if afraid to get inside or look Etta in the face.

"Can I ask you something, Miss Solis?"

"Of course," said Etta gaily. "And call me Etta, like everyone else.

"Yes, Miss Sol... Etta."

"Tell me, what is it you need?"

"I'd like you to instruct me if I do anything wrong." Reina looked up with her deer-like eyes, but looked down immediately. "Raul said you are the one to turn to."

Etta put the tablet down and came to the girl, uplifting her head by the chin.

"I will always help you," she said in a mild voice. "But why have you came to me and not to Leonid Derkacz or Doctor O'Leary?"

"Because they are both too busy and important. They shouldn't be disturbed with some unimportant matters.

"Come and sit." Etta dragged the quest to her bed. "Tell me, why do you think you are doing anything wrong? There must be a reason, isn't there?"

"I think... I think that humans are afraid of me."

Etta sighed. She understood the problem all too well and knew that solving it was going to be a drudge.

"Did Derkacz tell you why humans cannot be harmed?"

"Sir Derkacz said many things. I do not understand some of them. I do not harm."

"What about McBride? You almost broke his hand."

"It was necessary. The captain cannot be disobeyed. It was for McBride's own good."

"Good, Reina, cannot be done by violence."

"I don't understand. Never?"

Etta went silent. She suddenly realized that there was not any valid answer to this question. Pulling a child's arm can cause the pain, but what if it is the only way of preventing it from falling from the cliff? Repairing teeth used to be painful, but did doctors cease to do it? Sometimes clustered leg must be cut off to drug a person from the crash. It is extremely painful but it is the only way to save a life. How could Etta explain that to the android to make sure she would get it right? Reina's hands were so thin, tiny and soft, it was hard to believe how strong they could be.

"I will give you the answer: pain, with a good intention, can only be inflicted to a human by a human. Androids like you can make a mistake, because you do not know our physiology as well as we do. There is one exception for you: if anyone meant to do harm to the captain, you can stop that person. You must do it then. And tell me now, had your first Dominant beat his wife and children?"

"Only when they deserved it. He always said that it was for their good, to let them know they did wrong."

"I see. Dario is a bad man, Reina. His... logical circuit is broken. I know that you tried to help forcing McBride to talk. But don't do such things, evermore. Let humans deal with their own matters."

"But if anyone tried to break captain Kirk...?"

"That's the exception." Etta wasn't sure she was making the right choice, but she had to let Reina protect the captain, just in case. "Did you understand all I've said?"

"Yes, Miss Solis, Etta."

"Just Etta is fine. You can always come to me if you have any more questions. I want you to think of me as your friend."

Reina was silent for a while. Her sweet face was still, only the lashes trembled slightly, the eyelids stirring. She has heard the word, but couldn't find it in her data.

"F-R-I-E-N-D," Reina spelled slowly, and cocked her head. "Can I have human friends?"

"Yes, you can," Etta confirmed. "Me and Rasmus are friends, aren't we? It's not as close as the relationship with a companion, but it is still nice and important. And I really like you, Reina."

"So, if we are friends, I have one more favor to ask you," said the droid shyly. "Would you teach me some housework and body massage techniques?"

It was like an unexpected blow between the eyes.

"Sure. But what for?" Etta asked.

"I've heard doctor Xiao talking to corporal Svensen, that the captain deserved the real girlfriend, the one who could do all that. So I want to learn everything. For Kirk's well-being."

Etta touched Reina's cheek, feeling the soft, artificial skin. She felt she had to protect her, maybe after seeing her ling like a broken mannequin in some abandoned storage. And maybe she just felt ashamed, because she could do something to alter Reina's poor faith, but didn't. Wasn't Dario Cantoralle Etta's brother-in-law?

"I will teach you," Etta promised. "You will learn everything. But tell me, why have you chosen the captain in particular?"

Reina cocked her head again and grimaced with something that could be called a smile.

"He was the one to choose me," She said. "No. It wasn't a matter of choice. When Derkacz said there was nothing more he could do for me, the captain looked at me and asked: Reina, would you like to be my Companion? I was never asked to agree to anything. He was the first one to ask."

Her voice was quivering slightly, even though Reina was talking in a casual mode.

All who claim that androids do not have any souls should hear that.

Kirk Willner had treated Reina as if she were a human, and she could appreciate that. And her gratitude evolved into real bond. Etta felt deeply touched, like in the moment when she realized for the very first time that Raul wasn't just a perfectly programmed machine, but a person who could think by himself and make his own decisions, having his own point of view on everything. She realized then that the droids weren't simply copying human behavior; they wove their own patterns from them. And Reina was here to confirm her theory.

***

Even though nobody said it aloud, everyone was wondering how the droids were managing the ferry. The simplest everyday tasks were slipping out of people's hands, they were all thinking about the captain, alone on the bridge. Even the cook prepared something unusual, which looked like gravel, was hard as a rock but at the same time turned out to be surprisingly tasty. He just confused the temperature button with the humidity button, and it resulted in crystallizing some of the sugars in the protein mass, creating some crispy, sweet chips. Larson just saved it in his data base, not wanting to admit that the new dish was a result of his lightheadedness. Everyone enjoyed the new dish, so it was scheduled into the regular menu.

And Kirk Willner was seated alone, separated from the rest of the bridge by a soundproof panel; listening to humming and buzzing of the communication module. None of the droids thought of contacting him during the flight. They had nothing to report, they didn't need any extra instructions, and so they remained silent. It took them eight long hours to finally send a call.

Kirk Willner pushed the receiver button.

"Rescue, team, report!"

It was Raul's distorted voice that answered.

"We can see the refugee ferry."

"Details?"

"The engines are dead. It is visibly damaged by a rock crumb, many of those are cruising through the space here. They do not answer our calls."

"Can you get inside without a hazard for live forms?" the captain asked and murmured to himself: "What am I asking them to do?"

After a short break Raul spoke again:

"We can shoot a sleeve at the emergency door and open it with a decoding key."

The sleeve was a seemingly old-fashioned device of a folded material that could put its magnetic mouth around any steel surface and create a hermetic space inside, a safe passage that could be filled with breathable air. Everyone could work with the sleeve, but it was only a simulation on earth. Even the Captain didn't know how it would feel to crawl through the sleeve with only a thin cloth dividing him from the icy, biting, never ending void outside. Fortunately the androids didn't know fear, couldn't be altered by panic. Whatever happened, they would work logically. He only prayed for their logic to work right.

"Attention, the rescue team! Consult all your progress with me, unless it causes the delay hazardous for the passengers of the ferry. Do you read me?"

"Consult the actions that do not need an immediate progress." Raul paraphrased. "We are preparing the sleeve to launch."

"Proceed."

Willner dreamed of a camera showing the droids' doing. None of Vikings equipment could track such a small particle as the ferry, in such a long distance. He could see only green dots on the screen, among the bigger red dots indicating the floating rocks.

The captain projected the picture on the map and realized what must have happened. The comet cruising nearby disfigured the rock field. The licensed pilot would definitely correct the course, but Warens thought that setting the auto-pilot according to the data he had was enough.

"He could at least put it into dynamic mode," murmured Willner.

He wasn't angry, only frustrated. The man was not thinking logically, he was like a madman with flashes of consciousness He believed in technology, but didn't want to be indecisive. And the dynamic mode wouldn't allow him to take the steers, it would lead the ferry straight from point A to point B, without waiting for any human decisions.

Raul spoke again:

"Captain, we have boarded the ferry."

"What's the situation?"

"The outer shell is hermetic, but it is concave where the rock must have hit it. The air parameters are normal, but the temperature is low. Engineer Warens is in the pilot seat. Wait a while."

In the silence Willner could hear some conversation in the distance, as if the android placed the microphone off his lips. Then Raul spoke again.

"Warens is dead."

"Are you sure?"

"Positive. No basic parameters, no breathing, no pulse, eyes opened and still, pupils unresponsive. Bodily fluids dried round his lips and on his clothes. Rigor mortis."

"Well, he cannot be more dead..." the captain murmured, and spoke to the mic: "Are you sure that the raft is hermetic?"

"Positive. Ruslana is checking the hibernation capsule now. The indicators are broken, we cannot say if the passengers are alive."

"Hook the ferry up and come back here, but slowly, you cannot overload the capsule. Maybe the passengers can be saved. There is nothing more you can do there. Land on Viking 02, where doctor Gongadze will wait for you with his crew."

"Yes, sir."

The autopsy told that Warens hit the steering console when the ferry sped up and then slowed abruptly. He supposedly died ten hours before the rescue team arrived, but it was imprecise due to the hypothermic atmosphere inside the raft. The same episode crushed the thermostat and hibernation capsule. It was opened in an emergency mode in Viking 02, but it was too late to save Leila Sabatini. The petite brunette died, her Eastern features frozen in a calm way forever. Gongadze managed to re-create the course of events: the crush turned the emergency waking process. The oxygen Leila was breathing was infused with an anesthetic, and she partially woke up. Taking the mask off, she choked on the liquid filling the sleeping tube and drowned.

It was almost no better with six month old David. The doctors managed to resuscitate and stabilize him, but they were far from celebrating.

"It's too early to cheer," said doctor Xiao while the sum up meeting. "The baby is in critical state. His lungs are damaged and due to temporary lack of oxygen retinopathy might occur. He could be permanently crippled if he survives this. I am not sure if we should keep him alive in that case."

"He could, but we cannot state that he would," opposed Etta.

"The risk is high," Linde agreed with his colleague. "We are doing what we can, but-"

"We are. But I doubt there is a sense in keeping the crippled one alive."

"Why do you want to kill that little one so much?" sneered La Ver. He was standing leaning against the wall, with his arms crossed against his broad chest. He was eyeing the gathering as if keeping some guard upon them.

Xiao froze.

"I am a certified doctor, with an A3 job qualification certificate," she answered coldly. "I am not willing to explain my decisions to any soldier!"

"You don't have to excuse yourself, but do you have to put the baby to sleep?"

"You'd rather have him suffer?"

"You are exaggerating, doctor. He is unconscious, so he isn't suffering. And a chance that he would be healthy is still there."

"And what can you know about it?"

"Order!" demanded the captain. "Is this a primary school? Miss Hornet, you were about to speak, I noticed?"

The eyes of all gathered, including people in the screens, turned to Veronica, who cleared her throat, all shy suddenly.

"What I am about to say is a global secret, but we are not on the globe anymore, so I guess I can ignore that fact. Long ago the technique of reversing the breeding block in zero specimen was invented. Demography Department says that after re-introducing people to the areas which are now contaminated, but soon won't be anymore, and after producing more food we could think of producing more births..."

"What births? Crippled?" cried Xiao passionately.

"Not necessarily. Maybe physically weakened, but ready to function on their own."

"And what for, if I may ask?"

Veronica sighed. It was not easy to talk about such matters, but she had already started and intended to continue.

"I don't know if you have noticed one simple fact: our society is still developing scientifically and technically, but in some fields we are only copying things that had been done before. We haven't invented anything really innovative in years. The arts are declining. There are no poets, painters or sculptors among us. The only art we have is the one we had inherited. And it is so because we, as a species, eliminate the ones whose body may be weaker, but whose sensibility and imagination might be stronger. The nature works like that: if one has healthy body and precise mind, that one is unlikely to become an artist. Being an artist may be a result of compensation what body lacks. The constant struggle with weakness creates artistic potential. And art is the only thing that distinguishes us from animals, ladies and gentlemen. So the Department hopes that after the resources are back, we could loosen the genetic-clear breeding a bit and therefore produce some new visionaries, painters and poets."

"Bull-shit!" sneered doctor Linde, and MacLean O'Leary only raised his eyebrow.

"That's no bull-shit at all," he said in a calm voice. "Milton got blind in early age. Toulouse-Lautrec was a hideous cripple, Guy de Maupassant was mentally distorted. James Watt's body was so weak that the man constructed first steam engine wanting to help it move. And what about Steven Hawking, that brilliant astrophysicist from the break of the centuries? He couldn't speak or move, and it didn't prevent him from understanding the universe and state the theories about it. And there were many more like them. I bet no artist was fully physically and mentally healthy. We have created the society of physical perfection, which is no more than a swarm of insects. And we lack the most important ingredient: the spiritual one."

"So what are you suggesting? Creating an asylum of crippled individuals infused with the government money and observing if any talent of spoiling the canvas with the brush occurs?" asked Ian Callum. O'Leary only smiled faintly.

"Mister Callum, you are the product of our age, indeed! Just imagine you've lost your leg or arm without a chance of replacing it with cybernetic one. I bet it would make you lose your sanity, or even bring you to suicide! And not so long ago people with such defect were not only thriving: they worked, laughed and created. I have seen the paintings done with the brushes moved by lips or toes, by people with no arms. And they did this because they lacked artificial hands. The blind ones used to read by touching little dots printed on paper, they moved around with the help of white canes or specially trained dogs. They hadn't even dreamed of the cameras sewn into places where they eyes used to be. But they didn't break, they continued, and they were much stronger than we are now. And many of the devices that are so obvious for us now were created to compensate some lack of an artist or a person close to his heart."

O'Leary's speech produced such fuss that the captain had to stand up and banged his fist on the table to get some attention. People were aroused, shocked. The theses of Veronica and O'Leary were opposed to what they had been taught for years, since they were conscious enough to understand. And now those theses were a treat to the order they had known through all their lives. The captain's intervention brought some peace and Veronica could continue:

"You have misunderstood me, my fellows. What I mean is protecting some weak children that are produced nowadays. And this does not happen so often. Such child will grow up weak but self-sufficient. But the mind in such body could outgrow everything we know now."

"Let me cut in," Etta said. "I know the phenomenon Veronica is talking about. It is not new in the history of humankind. A long time ago there was a country called Sparta. And the citizens there had such high standards in terms of health that only the strongest babies were allowed to live. It resulted in producing a society of warriors that was conquered by the nation of philosophers, artists and scientists: the Greeks. And it was so because the Spartans lacked minds who could produce new and innovative war strategies, who could make their weapons more efficient. They lack creative, imaginative minds. They had though plenty of strong soldiers who could follow orders without giving them a second thought. They had eliminated all their potential leaders right after birth, when they were born crippled. So, Sparta had been brought down by weak geniuses, even though it had the healthiest and strongest warriors.

A brief silence fell.

"Those were different times, when everyone fought with everyone. There are no wars now..." said Callum. "Our situation now is different."

"Indeed. But it is not good to forget what it means to be a human. The clean-breed system seems to work perfectly, but I think it is too tight. I am a primary teacher. And during my practice I haven't seen even one child who could produce a drawing saying that it has an open, creative mind. They were all narrow, scientific minds, like computers. They could learn by heart, but without understanding. It was the result of acetylcholine supplementation, some parents could allow that. But none of those kids could create anything, even the simplest rhyme or story, even though they enjoyed listening to those. And those are the effect of our effecting the evolution. We only care for those physically perfect and mentally stable. And some time ago we used to say that every individual matters. Every single one."

"I bet that was why so many of them died of hunger, in poverty and dirt." Gongadze murmured sarcastically.

Doctor Xiao licked her small, plump lips.

"Let's say that there are some rights in what you are saying. Does it mean that we should sacrifice all we have achieved for those old-fashioned ideals? Do I have to remind you the price we have paid for reckless breeding?"

"Of course not!" Veronica replied. "It only means that we shouldn't cancel the one whose brain reminded untouched."

"That's true. The brain wasn't damaged in any way."

"So let's give him a chance. He will have some difficulties with breathing but he doesn't have to be an athlete, does he? If his eyes are bad, I will construct sight implants for him myself. We have all the parts needed, and I know how to do it. This is what we do when somebody lost the ability to see, dammit!"

"Well, we do..." Doctor Xiao hesitated and looked at Tenzig Gongadze, as if asking him silently, but he only shrugged.

Perhaps he was thinking of little Timmy, his own son, and thanked whatever gods he remembered that he was not the one who had been kidnapped. It could have as well been his son, and this whole congregation would decide now about the termination of his life. He shook those considerations off.

"I think we can as well wait," he said cautiously, "Lung damage is not so serious as to make ventilation critically impossible in the future. And if we consider the sight, we can fix it, even here. But if further problems occur, I will be the first one to vote for the termination. There are limits, especially in our present situation."

The captain rolled his gaze over the congregation.

"So?" he asked. "It means we are giving the boy a chance?"

Some whispers rustled and the decision was to give it a try till the conditions alter. And they off they went, all relieved but not eager to say it. Termination of weak infants was a common practice that was to provide the society with only healthy and strong babies, but deep inside people did not accept it. That was why the pre-conception and prenatal tests were so strict. It was easier to provoke a miscarriage than to kill a crippled baby.

X

The next fortnight was filled with gossip of little David's health. He was fighting for his life and the doctors didn't leave his bed. They panicked or became euphoric, as if not remembering their plans of terminating the boy's life. Food technicians had their own problems to solve: what to feed the baby with once it is not fed with the drops anymore? Nothing they had was meant for babies, so they had to synthesize proper mixture for him, not only nutritious, but also with a taste that would suit his needs.

We all hope David Sabatini would survive. Winning the battle for his life is just a start of our crusade. We have to take care of him and keep him well till some chosen colonists would take those responsibilities as his foster parents. We still cannot foresee how much damage his condition suffered.

Etta ceased to write.

Nobody could calculate that.

Even though the expedition had the best doctors and equipment, it was loaded somewhere in the bowels of the ships and used after they landed. Ambulatories had only essential emergency equipment for adults. Luckily they managed to use some of those to sustain the boy's breathing and circulation. With no hyperbaric cabin the doctors just manipulated the air pressure in a primitive oxygen tent. Nobody could be sure though that it would be enough to sustain the petite body.

Suddenly the boy became "the son of the army" and none of the crew was uninterested in his well-being. Even cynical O'Leary was there every day to ask how he was doing. Doctor Xiao, sneering at the experiment and openly admitting she didn't like babies, was doing all she could to help David.

But what would they do if the boy was to be seriously crippled? Whom would he become? Even though Etta wrote her master's thesis on her brain-body dependence and won a Tacit Prize for it, she was not so sure they would work in practice. She has proven, analyzing the biographies of great authors' that the writers' block was caused by messing with breeding processes of humankind. Elimination of damaged genes caused decrease in creative imagination. People didn't feel the need to compensate their disadvantages with made up stories and characters. The only readable stories were cliché romances and criminal stories in which all the readers knew who were the killer even before they were half way through the story. The self-improvement guides and scientific section was flourishing. People craved for the literature of past ages, reading through electronic libraries archives, but nobody was able to produce literature of that kind anymore. Was it really caused by the absence of fragile bodies and sensitive minds?

Etta sighed deeply.

She answered the knock on the door and let captain Willner inside. He rolled in heavily, his eyes were circled with black, face shrunk; he looked tired all over.

"Writing about the baby, right?" he asked, sitting next to Etta.

"I have to. It is a chronicle, isn't it?"

"It is. I... I am not quite sure if I'd made the right decision. I'm afraid it is too early."

"Too early for what?" Etta looked at the captain flabbergasted. He was sitting with his head hanging low, not as a charismatic leader of a space convoy would.

"People are not ready to change their ways of thinking. The lecture on Sparta had moved them, but it is not enough."

"They are confused. They are afraid that someone pulling the strings up there would like to restore the wild breeding. I am quite sure that it would not come to that, but even I was touched by Veronica's revelations."

"You shouldn't be. New regulations are to be applied only in case of the border liners, just to check if the system would work. If the statistics are favorable, we will all gain something. It is for the common good, and the decrease in the number of births is no longer demanded."

"The boarder liners" were people whose breeding abilities wavered between zero and one. Nobody was sure how to mark them, so they were marked as zeros, just in case. And they became the outsiders, just like all zeros were.

"Shitty life!" the captain looked at Etta with sheer desperation in his gaze. "Have you ever wanted a family? A babies born of you?"

"That sounds like a rhetorical question!" she whispered. "Why would I care to work in a primary school? I love kids, but nevertheless I will never become a mother. I am not allowed to. I am like a fruitless apple tree."

Willner just hugged her and crushed her to his broad chest.

Raul was standing at Etta's door. People just passed him, but he was poised, following their every move.

"And what about us?" asked Raina, standing close to him. Her deer-like eyes seemed almost human. "What happens to us if they become a couple? They won't need us anymore!"

"They will," Raul answered. "Believe me, they will always need us. They are not as the rest of humans. We are their equals in their eyes, they treat us as if we are their friends."

"They will abandon us."

"They won't. You just cannot get what humans are all about, Raina."

The android just turned her head no.

"I don't," she admitted.

Raul nodded.

"I noticed that some time ago. I will give you Rivas's book on human behaviorism. It should help you build relationships with them."

"But I..."

"What?"

"I can't read."

If Raul were capable of surprising, he definitely would be surprised in that moment. Being an android he was only vaguely wavered in his stream of consciousness.

"Hasn't Derkacz noticed that?"

"He had never asked me if I could. And he never let me read anything. We were only talking."

"That's a minor problem, easy to make up. We are designed to learn fast. I will teach you to read myself."

"I thought I was forbidden to learn."

"No, you aren't, you are bound to learn. If we are to be useful the ability to read is essential."

"My first dominant thought different." Raina's face remained blank.

"Just forget about it."

"You know all too well I cannot."

"I know. It is just the saying. It means: do not waste your time thinking about it. It is all past. Your Dominant is Kirk Willner now, and he does not forbid you a thing, does he?"

Raina was silent.

"Well, what is he like?" rushed Raul, and then she lifted her gaze at him.

"He never shouts. His way of speaking to me is different than that of master Cantoralle and master Derkacz. The captain is whole different than they are. He... he acknowledges me. I don't want to leave him. When I am with him, everything is as it should be."

"So, you have created the bond you lacked with your previous dominants. You were a target for the first one, and a Mission to accomplish to the other. And for the captain you are the real Companion."

They both went silent, until Rasmus approached them. His precise mind was already stable after the Kovac's doppelganger's attack, but he had some gaps in the memory. Doctor O'Leary said that it was due to the damage to some irreplaceable anemones.

"I'm looking for the captain," he said.

"He's at my Domina's," Raul stated. "If it is not an urgent matter you can wait here."

"I will. Veronica ordered me to come back at dinner time. She has an appointment with major LaVer."

"Are they together now?"

"I suppose so. They are together quite often nowadays."

"Does the major accept your presence?" asked Raina.

Rasmus seized her with his amber eyes as if surprised.

"I just go out when he comes. I am not in anyone's way."

"I mean, does the major wish... you weren't Veronica's Companion anymore?"

"Why would he care about me? I'm only Veronica's assistant, I work with her."

"But a human likes to be the only owner."

"And what does it have to do with us?"

Suddenly Raina shuddered, as if a powerful electrical shock hit her. Then she froze and her eyes became dull like some dolls.

"Why the hell have you dragged it here?" she barked with changed voice. "You need a plastic lover? You have a family! Either she stays in this house or me!"

"Raina..."

"Shut up! I am the boss here and it is going to be my way! You want me to punish you? Is that what you want?"

Raul lifted his communicator.

"Doctor O'Leary, it is Raul 209C. We have a problem here that needs your intervention. We are at Etta Solis's door. Could you please come to assist us?"

"I'll be right there!" answered O'Leary.

He soon appeared, disheveled, barefoot and with his uniform unbuttoned. One could see he has just got out of his bed.

"What's up?" he asked.

"Something is wrong with Raina."

The doctor looked at the droid, who just stood motionless and seemingly blind, totally unresponsive.

"What did you say to her?" he asked, producing a small torch out of his pocket, directing its beam into the android's eyes.

Raul just re-told the conversation, modifying his voice to imitate the characters. Remembering everything in detail was one of the most useful android's feature.

"Hmmm... We have an information incompatibility here. Some of it is from the period of shaping of the personality, and some of it is present. Anthropologists call it the dogma conflict. She is disoriented, doesn't know what to save and what to delete."

"Is she lagged?" asked Rasmus.

"Fortunately, she isn't. She is just... confused. We will fix her in no time Just keep an eye on her."

O'Leary rushed to his quarters and came back with a device that looked like an ancient walkie-talkie. It was a complicated thing used only by cybernetics. They gave the android direct suggestions using it. O'Leary fitted the frequency carefully and said to the microphone:

"Raina, whatever your first Dominant had said to you, is now invalid. Everything you hear from now is prior to what you had heard so far."

Raul and Rasmus covered their ears to change the doctor's voice into an incoherent flow of sound. They were not supposed to acclaim his words for prior order.

Not many specialists had such equipment and knew the frequency that would make the whole procedure work.

Hearing the order Raina ceased to stare mindlessly, blinked and looked at the doctor, who messed her curly hair.

"It is all right now, girl!" he said.

"Why hadn't Derkacz used such a device when he reclaimed Raina?" asked Rasmus.

"It is being used just in extreme cases, because it is said to be slightly ethical." O'Leary switched the device off. "The law is far behind the technological development. Anthropologists had to design their own code of law, because only they know that androids are not some complex machines, but conscious creatures."

The doctor recalled the memoirs of Henry Karpinsky he had read not so long ago.

I was shocked this morning. Mark L34, when placed at the mirror, pushed his hair up so as to look more like me. I gave him the comb and he used it, slightly awkwardly. It seems L34 has crossed the borderline. He now knows that the object reflected in the shiny surface is himself. And it means that he has the idea about his own self.

"What can be unethical in helping one of us?" asked Raul, and the doctor was visibly surprised that his words had been comprehended that way.

"The point is," O'Leary said after a while, "that using this device an anthropologist can control the behavior and mind of an android. And that is morally wrong."

"Why? Even if it is to help?"

"It is a highly abusive method! People don't even know that such a device exist and it better stays this way, because-" he stopped abruptly as a nurse appeared in the corridor.

"I have some bad news about David Sabatini," he said. "Have you seen the captain?"

This time it took thirty six hours to stabilize little boy's condition. The whole medical team of Viking 02 was fighting fiercely for the baby's life, saying that if the decision of sustaining it was mad, they couldn't just give up right now. The anxiety took over the ships, nobody slept for a day and a half, waiting for any news from the medical center. Even doctor Xiao was waiting for it, even though she repeated time after time "I told you!" She was more nervous than anyone could suspect. O'Leary has found her weeping at her desk.

"Are you so worried about the brat's health?" he asked, obviously surprised by her poor condition; he clearly didn't expect that.

"Of course I am! Do you really think I am heartless?" the Chinese started to sob uncontrollably and he had to comfort her for a long time.

But, fortunately, death decided once more to withdraw and the doctors sighed with relief. The condition of little David was better with each passing moment and all teams could go back to their chores, which they had abandoned lately. And they had discovered one more thing: John Warens was a nobody, no one could find any information on him, just some unimportant trivia.

"It's more than enough!" the captain shouted, reading the information. "Do they put only idiots in the inner control department? First the fraud that claimed to be Kovacs, and now this!"

"Some tough hacker must have messed up with those data," explained Pavlov, the chief of I.T. department. "Vanka and Casseres are working on regaining some of those."

"Any clues?"

"None so far. As soon as we have anything I will let you know."

One thing was sure: John Warrens was no saboteur. What was more probable was that he had been the unregistered passenger who got scared by the size of the venture. He was no fraud. His DNA was found in the data base, but no details had been provided on him. He was born, he graduated from some school and... that was it. No data on training or jobs. Only after Warens enlisted in Crew Department some notes appeared. And after a couple of nights of intense work the I.T. technicians found something that astonished them. It turned out that the man's real name was Gianni Sabatini and he had been the husband of deceased Leila.

"Well, he used to be, at least," Vanka concluded to the captain. "They were divorced. He had legally changed his name shortly before enlisting to the Crew Department, stating that he didn't want anything to remind him of his ex-wife. He wasn't sentenced, no mental illnesses, good student and intern, so it was easy for him to finalize that."

"Was Leila enlisted for the colonization program first?" the captain asked.

Vanka searched for the needed info on his touch pad.

"Then weeks earlier. Two weeks before Sabatini asked for the name change."

Willner just bowed his head.

It was no sabotage this time, no nonprofessional deed of anyone. It was just the man who tried to save his wife and son, and the one who should have been pitied. He tried to work reasonably, but his conclusions were false and the outcome quite pathetic.

At least the little one survived... thought the captain, "but unfortunately the mother is gone."

"One more issue, captain," Vanka disturbed his thoughts. "We have some information on the false Kovacs. They have checked out his identity. His real name is Ivo Hasek and he originated in New Zealand Golden Praha. He was in the Hiperpotencial Children Special Education program, the one for the kids with high IQ. Licensed pilot, dismissed due to his unstable, conflict prone personality. He didn't agree for the therapy. Arrested twice for sabotaging."

"Quite a persona. Anything else?"

"Isn't that enough, captain?"

Willner was brooding. If the captive was so intelligent, maybe his mind could have been changed? He would make a valuable member of the colony. He could have been pushed through some intense psychotherapy techniques, but the captain didn't like the extreme. He despised the messing with anyone's psyche, no matter the situation, and he wasn't willing to do than, even though his medical team had the essential drugs and equipment to proceed with it.

"Why wouldn't you do that, captain?" asked Veronica when he confided in them during the lunch. "Those are safe and commonly accepted procedures."

"When I was but a lieutenant, one of my colleagues murdered his wife, he stabbed her out of jealousy," said the captain in a gloomy voice. "He tried to save her, though, called an ambulance, so he had been given a choice: termination or some hard psychotic mess up. He chose the further. And they had made a cripple out of him. He works in some small utility for former prisoners, he is afraid of open space, he doesn't make eye contact, no joy, no interests. When he doesn't work, he just sits on the bench, drinking can beer and staring into space. It is not life, it is vegetation. He used to be an energetic man, he loved climbing, and he was a member of a hockey team, winning some competitions every week. I visited him once after the procedure. I wasn't eager enough to visit him again."

"Well, he was the murderer," mumbled Etta.

"And what they had done to him was also a homicide, if anyone asked me. I am not an ideal man, but I have my rules and I stick to them. And a human personality, even if it is wicked, monstrous, is something sacred to me. And if anyone is to be executed, it should be done respectfully, treating such person with dignity, as it is a whole, separate human being. And those methods erase the dignity."

"Some humans are humans only of name."

"They surely have. And I think they should be eliminated. But not changed into mindless beasts or keep them in a cage where they would become beasts. It puts us, as a species, in a very bad light."

"And we, as a species, used to think that nobody's life should be taken. It was a basic rule in almost every society." Etta spooned the rest of her meal out and put the cutlery down. "It was said that the law cannot be over that basic rule, that if a single person cannot kill, so cannot the law system. No killing meant no killing. And it took centuries to validate the "social tissue operation act". And the point in the New Constitution saying that the murderer is just a cancer who must be removed for the sake of the whole body, was fiercely attacked at the beginning of the New Era."

"People just didn't know what was good for them." Veronica looked at the portion of hot mash and made a sour face. "I'm fed up with this crap! Larson tries hard, but everything tastes the same. Like crap! And it smells alike! If there is any spare capsule left, I will gladly lie down in it!"

They were all fed up with poor quality food and stinking water, that came from the self-purifying close circuit. The atomic collectors were not efficient enough. Fresh water was a delicacy, and in little amounts. Everyone tried not to nag. And androids were privileged in some matters: they didn't need to eat nor drink, they didn't need to breathe even. And the cosmic radiation was of no harm to them. People knew that even though there were protection screens on the outer shells of the crafts, some radiation penetrated. That was why only "zeros" had been recruited as a space crew. They didn't have to worry about the radiation damaging their glands and at the same time damage their future offspring. The colonists in the capsules were better protected: they were isolated by the covers of the capsules made with thermoplastic lead infused material, and the fluid inside. They were sound asleep, anyway. They didn't have to suffer the drudge of the journey, eat the crappy food, and when they would wake up, they wouldn't even know how long their lethargy lasted.

"Nobody puts you in the capsule, we need you," murmured the captain. "And if it is of any consolation to you, our food is still better than in the army."

"Was it really that bad?" Etta dropped in, as the conversation was heading towards the topic that was of her interest, and that was the military, so often ignored by the civilians. Even though they were protectors of the humankind, they were best forgotten.

"The soldiers must train both their minds and bodies. There is no gluttony in the army. We had some extra meals only on holidays. And every day menu was a bowl of soup, some concentrates and dried meat substitute. It tastes like cardboard, but it has only needed ingredients and no toxins," explained Willner. "A soldier must be healthy, so he doesn't eat anything potentially poisonous. And we tend to favor not the food that is good for us: salt, sweets and fat.

"Have mercy, captain!" Veronica sighed painfully. "I would kill for a fatty meat chop and ice-cream! I am not a soldier type!"

"End who is?" Etta rested her chin on her hand. "I used to wonder, what does a recruiting procedure look like?"

Kirk Willner just smiled.

"They just come to us. Those who have the will, they find the way. And believe me, there are many."

Veronica raised her eyebrows.

"Really?"

"Really. You two, well, you are both zeros, so you have been through drudge, but you were raised under a glass pane. Your parents were from the privileged social class, you had no problems with getting into university. You had no worried about paying your bills. Not everyone lives in such comfort."

Etta didn't reply, but she knew what the captain was talking about. The citizens from the outskirts, where the working class was located, were the ones with lower IQ, and therefore couldn't work in exposed sectors. Etta always thought they were not treated right. Poor jobs meant poor salary and poor food ratios.

And if the children were more intelligent than the parents, it was not easy to provide for them during their studies. Some had to work and learn at the same time. Did most soldiers come from that social class?

"Many recruits just cannot see any meaning to their existence," continued the captain. "If a married couple decides to enlist, their kids are automatically enlisted and being brought up like future soldiers. It is the same with the police. Your lives, my ladies, was always meaningful, so it may be hard for you to grasp that."

Corporal Svensen approached their table.

"Sorry to interrupt you, captain, but the Kovac's doppelganger wants to talk to you."

"High time!" Veronica sneered, and the captain silenced her with a cold gaze.

"I'll be right there," he said, getting up. "I made this urchin read some original source materials, maybe he made up his mind."

"Maybe," Veronica murmured, putting some more food into her mouth.

She would gladly abandon the meal half-way through, but she knew well enough that her body needed the food, even though it tasted like crap.

Kirk Willner entered Kovac's room, which has been turned into a cell for a time being. Well, he was really Ivo Hasek, and even though he had caused so much trouble, the captain felt kind of sorry for him. Many crew members felt claustrophobic, and this one here had to suffer from enclosure even more. He couldn't even go for a walk through the corridors. But the captain was not willing to risk letting the saboteur run free.

"You wanted to talk to me?" the captain asked from the door, in his most stiff tone.

Ivo Hasek looked at him above his reading device.

"I surely did," he replied. "I wanted to ask you this all important question: Do you really believe that the colony can be established on that mythical planet? Let's assume for the need of this conversation that the planet exists."

The captain stepped into the Kovac's room, the door slid close behind him with a barely audible hiss. He was still looking at his interlocutor while sitting on a portable stool.

"This is a wrongly stated question," he said. "My beliefs have nothing to do with this journey. I was given an order and I am following it. But if you want to know my personal opinion..." The captain hesitated, he wasn't sure he should verbalize it, but the prisoner's eyes were piercing his conscience. "I personally think that even if Patris doesn't exist, we still have enough fuel to go back. But it is the unlikely scenario. If it wasn't for the Schoumaker's disc muting field, Jewel would have been discovered centuries ago. It was thought to be just a distortion of the signal for hundreds of years. But the technology speeds up and now we know that it is there, with the whole planetary system.

"We also know that it is not going to last long."

"It is long for our standards. Twenty five thousands of years is quite long for human kind. It is enough to find solutions for most of our major problems."

"Captain! We won't manage to reach anywhere! Biology and physics will prevent us from it! Going faster than light speed is theoretically possible, but no solid matter would survive it, if we were really to gain it. I was doing some calculations to kill my spare time, and the results are not making me happy. We are not going to manage to the borders of a Milky Way in one piece."

"Just leave it to the scientists, will you?" advised Willner. "We are only to establish a colony for our little group. It must be done if humans perish along with the Earth."

The prisoner looked as his small screen. He was pale, his eyes encircled in black.

"If the Earth perishes, there is nothing more to fight for and nothing more to live for," he said with a tiny voice, the sadness in it unbearable. And then he placed his face in his hands and cried bitterly.

Willner didn't know how to react, and he finally touched the man's shoulder.

"Our journey has nothing to do with the Earth's surviving, really," he said. "We are a kind or Holy Ark, a material for future generations, sent into space just in case. Have you read the Bible?"

The prisoner raised his head and looked at the captain with sheer surprise in his eyes.

"But it is a forbidden book! Only historians are allowed to read religious volumes!"

"Well, let's not be too secretive in the matter. People, especially young, are very fond of breaking the rules. So, have you read it or not? I do not ask officially."

"Only bits and pieces. My friend managed to get an unofficial copy of the first book."

"The story of Noe, do you know this one?"

"Yes."

"Let me show you something, then."

The captain moved to the vision connection panel and activated it with a four digit code. The screen flashed with a picture of something that looked like a huge chest of drawers, with multitude of tiny doors and blinking lights. Hasek looked at the screen, intrigued.

"What is it?"

"It is a freezer room. Each container has a genetic material of an animal or plant species inside. It is our ark. With the material there we can use any life-breeding species to breed the animals we had on Earth. If we find the creatures lying eggs, we can re-create our reptiles and birds. We can plant any planet with daisies, and make dragonflies and butterflies populate its meadows."

The captain touched the screen and another room appeared.

"And here we store the whole knowledge the humankind managed to accumulate throughout the centuries. The history of any civilization we managed to discover."

Hasek shrugged and stepped away from the panel.

"Without the equipment necessary to re-creating all those organisms your precious collection is useless," he said, sitting on his bed. "There are people who claim that the whole modern knowledge was presented to Stone Age humans by aliens. If they are right, think about the implications: they might have left anything, but the ancient cultures just couldn't decipher that.

What would ancient Greeks do with a pen drive? Wear it hung on a string as a necklace?"

"We have the devices, and the plans to make new ones, everything covered with extra durable plastic, and they are practically indestructible. If it is necessary we can chisel them in iron and stone, so the future generations would know what to do."

"Well, if a history takes a turn, in ten thousand years your plans would be perceived as some ritual paintings or some religious crap. Be serious. Two, three generations would be enough to take your civilization a thousand years back. Your genes and artifacts would be good for nothing, since nobody will be able to keep the fridge running."

"You are seeing everything in black, Hasek."

"Oh, so you already know my real name? Good for you, but it doesn't matter, really. A man is not a name, the same as your gathering here is no representation of a humankind. They may start something new if they are lucky, but I'm sure they won't. You can keep me here till I'm mad, but it won't save your people. They are all doomed."

The captain took a deep breath, counting to ten silently.

"That is your subjective opinion," he said after he cooled off. "Mine is different. But we can judge which one of us was right in a couple of decades. You have to realize that the colonists we gathered here are not some folks caught in the streets at random. They are highly qualified specialists of variety of professions. We planned everything, so the legacy of humankind could be protected, kept, and developed. People far wiser than you and me have been working on that for decades. Why can't you just trust in them?"

Ivo Hasek hesitated. He was clearly disturbed and didn't know how to respond to that. He had been bred in a pro-earth community, and his mind had been drenched in the idea of being loyal to his home planet no matter the cost of it. The organization he was a member made a huge effort so he could sabotage the space journey, and he failed. The convoy sped on, and he himself was being kept prisoner. His collaborates were more lucky and has been sent back. Hasek was the one who paid the highest price.

"Let me out of here, I won't be a trouble anymore," he finally begged, and the captain only looked at him sympathetically.

"I can't," he said. "The crew won't trust you anymore, and I cannot allow the paranoia to spread. You will remain here. We will let you go once we are in the colony."

"If we ever get there..."

The door slid aside and de Bernal appeared.

""Captain, we are approaching Kuiper's Belt in three hours."

Willner looked at his watch.

"We are! Just wait outside, we will go to the bridge together. And announce the meeting of the crew in a quarter."

The captain turned the vision panel off.

"Take a grip, Hasek!" he shouted at the prisoner. "I can ask the crew if they allow you to go for a walk from time to time. But nothing more."

"Yeah, that's what I dream of..." murmured the man, not even slightly happy with the idea.

XI

Most people from the crew had no idea what Kuiper's Belt even was. They were all educated in a very narrow areas, to create designed specialists in needed areas. The general education didn't include cosmology, and there was not even one astrophysician among them. Only the pilots knew what was there in the solar system and around it. Even Willner started to study astronomy once on the deck, and he gained some knowledge from the books collected on earth. His freshly absorbed knowledge allowed him to answer the multitude of questions from the crew now.

"The Schoumaker's Discus was named after the 20th century scientist. It is a part of Kuiper's Belt, with a multitude of other discuses, but contains a slightly different matter. It is a cluster similar to the planetoids gathering we can find between the Earth and Mars, but the objects forming Kuiper's Belt are mostly ice, not rocks, and those are frozen gases. Schoumaker's is completely different. It annihilates any signals, and that is why Jewel was hidden for so long.

"Is that true that the existence of a micro star so close to our solar system is against the law of physics that we know?" asked Ian Callum. His gray eyes were burning with curiosity.

The captain just shrugged.

"Our sun is just a dwarf star," he replied, "and its influence is relatively irrelevant. And Jewel is a real tiny object. The distance isn't the problem here, it is rather a fact that it even exists. No, I don't think it is against any known laws. It is the result of some law that we haven't recognized yet."

„I bet there are more than one!" O'Leary sneered.

He was the only one who didn't give a damn about any discus, micro stars and stuff like that. He accepted things as they were and didn't give them second thoughts. His mind was overwhelmed with tiniest matters, but nevertheless more relevant – the matters of A.I. The Androids were made to serve humans, but he was the one who – as a cybernetician – served them. He was breathing with the idea of helping those bastards of humankind, that weren't even perceived as living creatures. Of course, they weren't alive according to biological terms. Their bodies didn't feed and digest, they didn't breed. But it was the mind that was as agile as a human mind, and that one thing was enough to see them as living creatures. Those who were against said that Androids looked human, so some people wanted to treat them like humans.

One of the andropologists conducted a social experiment now known as Kappa-504. One of the persons who were awaiting for their Android Companion was granted only an artificial mind hidden in the colorful box with a loudspeaker. He was said that his permission to have a Companion was accidentally erased, and that was his gratification for a long period of waiting. After a while it turned out that the man was so bonded to his speaking box that he didn't intend to switch it to a typical android anymore.

Those were the problems dwelling in O'Leary's head. But he had to generate at least some interest of what was going on around him, as he was a passenger of a space ship heading towards the unknown planet.

„And if the discus really emits some kind of shield, how are we supposed to call the headquarters once we are engulfed by it?" the doctor asked.

Willner produced a holographic map of the area.

„This is the discus," the captain encircled a part of it with his laser pointer, „and here, just about a thousand miles from its Edge, is the automatic transmitting station *Michio 2*, that was launched to that spot before anyone started to check Patris. That is our eye. The rovers landing on the planed sent their data to the station, and *Michio* forwarded them to Earth. It was sufficient, so we can also use it."

„Can we? Does it work both ways?" asked Aisha Bahrani from her screen.

„Of course, engineer Bahrani, it would be useless otherwise."

„But how can we be so sure that the data sent back by the rovers weren't just made up?" asked Linde skeptically.

The captain knew that look on his youthful face all too well. After the Kovac's thing they had a coded call and Linde admitted that he used to be a member of The Green October agenda. He had many doubts still.

„It is not likely to be so," Willner stated. „When we reached *Michio*, I have downloaded all the data from its hard drive. It is all there, the pictures… Well, look by yourselves!"

He touched some buttons and the three dimensional screen flashed with trees just like those that used to grow on Earth, some green plains and mountains, and big lakes in the valleys.

„There are no oceans and seas on Patris, but we assume that some of the lakes are salty. It is a young planet, in its primal phase. The scientists think it was captured by Jewel's gravity field."

„Is it even possible?"

„Of course it is. Triton, one of the Neptune's moons, was magnetized like that from the rock belts surrounding the planet. The Earth was produced out of the materials spit out by the Sun, like some other planets of our solar system. But Jewel is a different kind of star, it hasn't got enough material to produce its own planets. Jewel here, we may say, adopted three huge rocks that became the planets finally: Ceserea, Patris and Eppia. Ceserea is the closest one to the star and it has no atmosphere, as it's too small to keep it. Patris is in the ecological belt, if I may name it like that, so it has perfect conditions for developing life forms. And as we all see, the life forms drink their full on its potential. Eppia is the biggest and the coldest. The gravity is two point five there, the atmosphere quite dense. There is a Chance of finding life forms there, but nobody bothered to look for it, as it is completely unsuitable for humans."

„Patris is beautiful!" whispered Cyra Lavell.

Tengiz Gongadze lifted little David, but the boy wasn't interested in admiring the planet that was to become his home. Others were spellbound and speechless. The only one who looked frustrated was Leonid Derkacz.

„We know nothing about the environment," he said. „We don't know what we will find there. Are we prepared for that?"

„We couldn't have been prepared more. We cannot foresee everything. We have scientific and medical equipment, we have engineering tools. We have our brains. We can adapt. And our own evolution as a species shows that our brains were better survival tools than fangs, claws and muscles, and even the quantity."

„Are there any big animals on that planet?" Bordem asked.

„We don't know that. Some big, complex organisms should have developed there, according to the air and soil samples, but there are no pictures of any animals thriving on the ground. We have a shot of some flying creatures that looks like the heard of birds, on the backdrop of clouds. So something lives there. We just don't know what it is."

„All of those rovers didn't manage to provide any answer?" Voznansky sounded surprised.

O'Leary burst with laughter.

„You may as well send a machine and a six-year-old kid on any planet, and we will see who finds life first!" he sneered. „Androids might have found something. But simple machines?"

„Androids couldn't have been sent there, and you know why! Thanks to people like you!"

„And I am proud of that outcome!"

„Cut it!" the captain interrupted the quarrel. „I won't tolerate personal engagement here! Any constructive questions, anyone? Our convoy is about to begin the procedure of speed reduction. We have to slow down, as the risk of hitting some objects is increased inside of the belt. The gravity will decrease, as it is dependent on the speed. It will fall to zero point five, and after the compressors adjust it...well, it will take about–„

„Twelve hours," engineer Ramsay from *Viking 04* finished for the captain.

„Yes. So please be careful and don't hurt yourselves. It's too easy to get bruised in low gravity."

After thirty minutes the process of slowing down began, and as O'Leary noticed it was thirty minutes too late. Everyone could feel the trembling of the ships as the first tiny rock particles started to rattle against the protective shields. The captain stood on the bridge all this time and scanned the monitors, at the same time peeking out of the vision slots to check if the ships were keeping the formation. It was the most dangerous part of the cruise so far. If the shields uncovered any part of the ship for just but a second at that speed, the rocks would pierce it for sure. And Willner hadn't believed it until he saw the demonstration at the high rank officers gathering at the Space Flights Centre.

„You don't need the light speed to make a damage," a tiny astrophysicist, a Japanese with a decreasing hairline was explaining, „Look at this: our Missile is just a candle, and the target is a two and a half inch thick board. And I have this device here that can make the candle go at the speed of sound."

„The candle will crumble!" one of the officers laughed.

The Professor smiled mysteriously, put a candle into the barrel of his device and pushed at the trigger. The blast was deafening, and the huge, tattered hole appeared in the board. The candle hung almost intact in the eladurex net behind it. The officers couldn't believe their eyes, they were passing the Missile from hands to hands. It was barely crushed at the top.

„As you can see, the power depends on the speed. And it doesn't matter what moves: the ship or the rock particles. They are both moving in vacuum, so we can name any of them the

185

mark, and any of them the missile. You will meet lots of moving objects in space. To make it clear: it doesn't matter if you toss a spear at the human being, or toss a human at the pointed spike. The damage will be done."

"But the weight of a man is bigger than that of a spear..."

"And the rule saying that object A influences object B with the force F...?"

"Gentlemen, we are talking about objects moving in the void. We have no gravity there that would affect the size of the damage... We are talking about space ships and space trash. If the ship goes on lower gear, the rock will just bounce off from its shell. But if the speed increases, such space trash can pierce the whole length of the vehicle. If we had no shields and nivelators, we would make no progress from the moment the first man manager to reach the moon."

The lecture was to help the captains realize that the shields were the crucial elements of their crafts. Their cost was one third of the whole shaft, and the technologies were the most advanced ones, more even than those used to build water collectors. The shields were nevertheless inspected by the captains twice a day and each of them shivered considering finding any abnormalities in them.

And now even the perfectly working collectors could be an insufficient protection. The convoy had to slow down. The critical moment was reaching the Schoumaker's Discus edge, where all the speakers would go mute and all the screens would go blank. The only way to communicate would be through the vision panels at the bridges, made of syntal – the top secret mixture of materials that provided almost hundred percent clearance, flexibility and damage resistance. It was hard to produce and extremely expensive, so only intergalactic cruisers had windows made of it.

Vikings were slowing down, reducing the speed to the second, than the first interstellar gear. The captain, looking straight ahead, with his hands clutched to the arms of his chair, realized too late that *Viking 04* broke the line and sped forward, ahead of the cavalcade.

"Zero four, what's going on? Hit the brakes now!" he shouted once he realized something was wrong.

The intercom buzzed and cracked, and finally they heard Titos Brazakis, the main pilot's voice:

"We can't! The steers are blocked! I'm going manual!"

"Switch the engines off, now!"

The speakers burst with the cacophony of multitude of voices, the pilots shouted trying to give some advice to *Viking 04*. Willner felt it lasted an eternity, even though the whole exchange took but a few seconds.

The unmanageable shaft drifted off and grazed a huge bulge of cosmic ice which punched it off the course, so it pivoted and slowed down. The right side of the craft wasn't shiny and smooth anymore, it was deformed, and the back of the stern blazed with overheated metal, then turned graphite black.

"All the ships, stop!" Willner shouted, "Rescue teams into ferries!"

He sped to the door, hit the opening panel and almost crushed into his people, all equipped and ready for the rescue Mission. They were zipping their overalls, their hands shaking with emotions. Only the androids were composed as ever, with their faces blank, which almost made Willner smile.

"I'm glad you are all here, but we don't need a whole pack. All the ships will send rafts so I'm taking corpora Svensen and-"

"Wait," LaVer interrupted, "you are the captain, you cannot take the risk."

Willner looked at him as if he hasn't understood.

"That is all regulated. And it is common sense. What would we do if you get hurt? We all depend on you."

"That is true," Willner nodded. "So you command the rescue team. Take Raul and Rasmus with you, and choose your human crew yourself."

Etta trembled. Even though she knew all too well how important her Companion was in this kind of a situation, she would gladly order him to stay put. She was as worried about him as she was worried about those people entombed inside a broken ship.

"I'm going with you!" she exclaimed before she realized how ridiculous it was.

Sherman LaVer looked at her with pity, she blushed under his gaze. How could she help: a petite, chubby face girl who looked like a child at the side of a two hundred and twenty pound, six feet tall man?

"No offense, but I need strong and crafted men. And you, Veronica, don't say a word! You are both in the army on some parity rules, but you are no soldiers."

"That wasn't nice!" Veronica sneered. "Be so kind and look after Brent."

"The droid's name is Rasmus. And he'd better take care of humans!" doctor Xiao barked. "The robots can take care of themselves. You take care after humans, I say! One human is worth a hundred of those, we can produce them! Why the hell do you call him Brent?"

"None of your business, but I will tell anyway. I named my imaginary friend Brent. And I started to call Rasmus that once I started to understand him. Why wouldn't an android have a regular name?"

"I will look after all my crew," said LaVer and looked at Xiao bitterly. "And you, doctor, don't get mad, because it can affect your pretty face!"

The chief of the rescue team howled to his troops and in a while Raul and Brent were gone.

"Do you realize that the slaves were being treated like that in the past?" said Etta to the doctor. "Only those who could be useful were being taken care of. The sick and wounded were being killed as useless."

"That is some bull-shit! Androids are no humans!"

"The blacks weren't considered humans in those days. They were called "Negroes" and the death of one was the loss of money."

"All silence!" The captain interrupted the quarrel when the Chinese was preparing a counter-strike. "We need to be focused now!"

It took but a matter of an assumed time for the rescue ferries to get to the door of *Viking 04*. The regulations stated clearly that no speeding was allowed in pace, even in emergency situations.

The professors always underlined that only living people could bring any help to those in danger. Even though the pilots were tempted to accelerate, the ferries crawled slowly to the broken ship.

The sleeves were shot out and after unlocking the doors the rescue crews stepped into the bowels of a seemingly dead craft.

The darkness inside was diluted by faint emergency lights and the spontaneous sparks flying from the cut electrical wires. The stench of melting plastic, chemicals fumes and dense smoke were another obstacles that couldn't be ignored and were hard to bare.

"Masks on!" LaVer barked, "And nobody takes it off until I say so, or I'll kick the hell out of you, no matter man or a woman!"

Only the androids didn't buckle the hoods around their heads. The crew members started to sneak through the compartments, guided by the commander. The main goals were to extinguish fires and evacuate the survivors. The rescuers from *Viking 02* were to take them over, as the main medical center was on their ship. The stunned people were being dragged out of their cabins and led through the sleeves. Those hurt were put on a portable stretcher which every rescuer had at hand. The androids headed to the engine room and passengers compartments while Sherman with two people went to see the bridge.

By some miracle the outer shell remained hermetic, but everything inside was rubble. Two pilots were kneeling there, too weak to stand up but trying to toss away the rubble blocking the way.

"Report, soldier!" LaVer shook one of them, and the man looked at him half-conscious, his eyes dull and blinded by blood.

"Brazankis dead, Denderry and Krasusky are still somewhere there."

"Are they alive?"

"I don't know, major."

LaVer made some inarticulate noise under his mask and started to help the men. Some rescuers arrived and the pilots were escorted away. One of the soldiers lighted the scene with his torch.

"Be careful, major!" he said. "If the rubble comes down, you might get stuck here as well."

"You be careful!" LaVer switched his head light on.

The small space was crumbled as if a giant palm had crushed it. In the beam of light there was a body resting in the untouched pilots cabin, hand still clutched on the main power cut out lever, head tossed back. That must have been Brazankis, who saved all of them by cutting the reactor off. He locked himself in by closing the emergency panels. The pressure broke one of the vision panels. The air was sucked out and also the pilot's life.

LaVer saluted to the body and scanned the room for the remaining men. They were both here: Sasha Krasusky crawling to his fours and coughing terribly, Denberry motionless under some broken steering console, blood dripping down the side of his head.

The major grabbed Krasusky and pushed him to the crack he made in the rubble.

"No protests! Get in and crawl away from here, I am the commander and the resistance will be punished by castration! Mori! Get him out to the shuttle!"

"What about you, major?" the soldier cried from the hole.

"Get out of here now!"

LaVer made to Denberry again. He was conscious and opened his eyes once major lifted his head.

"Sherman, my man!" he whispered faintly. "Why the hell are you here?"

"I am here for you! Let's get out of here!"

"Leave me, I am good for nothing anymore." the colonel moaned with pain while being lifted.

"Don't you give me this crap here! I would if I could, but in our present situation every man is precious. You know me and you know I am no altruist," LaVer tossed the body over his shoulder, ignoring the protests, "but your pitiful ass may be useful some day!"

The colonel was pushed through the crack carefully and handed to the rescuers.

"Don't go to the bridge, everything is rubble there! Report!"

"We have found everyone!" Kurosawa from *Viking 03* "The chief engineer Ramsay is dead, two technicians from his shift are in critical condition."

"One of the pilots is also gone," said LaVer, "but we cannot get the body now. What are the equipment loss?"

"It's bad, major. The air conditioning system dead, heating dead. It is not a matter of putting some patches on. It must be re-built."

"The passengers section?"

"Intact." It was Brent approaching. "Still air-tight, capsules all fine, the pressure normal."

With his statue-like composure, wearing no overalls and a trunk-like mask he looked the only human among the weird, glass-eyed, clumsy monsters.

"That's one good news. Are any AIs still working?"

"Yes, sir, they are helping the rescuers."

"Excellent! You stay with them and run the thorough diagnostics. I found one break in the pilots cabin, search for more. Patch the holes, clean the bridge and over all keep an eye on the capsules. That's it. We'll contact you soon."

XII

The thorough diagnostics left all with no illusions: it would take months and a specialized crew to make the ship fully functional again. The circuit sustaining the passenger's capsules was fortunately unharmed, and ATs have mended the reactor cooling system, so the engine could have been tested again. Aisha Bahrani reported it working after she finally came back to her own ship. Generating extra power managed the crew to use electro tools and steers. There was no place on the remaining *Vikings* for over two hundred capsules, they had to be transported to the planet surface on the broken craft. They did not have many other options. The air-condition and circulatory system were beyond fixing, the same with water recycling system. The heating and hydrogen collectors were also crushed. They barely managed to get to ten Celsius degrees.

"The cold is not as bothering as the fact that there is no air to breath." Bahrani concluded. "We must do something, cause we cannot leave the colonists here with no supervision."

"We won't. Any suggestions?" the captain asked.

"Is there no way to distribute them on the remaining crafts?" suggested doctor Linde.

"No damn way!" Woznansky sneered. "No place, no power to sustain the capsules. We barely managed to shelter the crew!"

O'Leary coughed and put his hands on the table in a steeple.

"Ladies and gentlemen, the thing is simple. No human can pilot the broken ship, even though the engine is fine and we

194

managed to fix all the holes to avoid further decompression. We cannot drag it, either, because it would hazard two ships involved. There is only one option."

"Don't you even suggest that!" Al Salazar, the pilot from *Viking 02*, protested. "You want an android to pilot the Zodiac-class ship?"

"Have you got any better idea?"

"No, but yours is ridiculous!"

"In our present situation even the ridiculous idea can save lives."

The gathering simmered. The quarrel between two camps broke and finally the captain hammered his tin mug with a knife to get some attention. He addressed Veronica:

"We already know that Rasmus can drive a ferry, but would he be able to pilot the *Viking?*"

All eyes turned to her, and Veronica patted her shaved head in embarrassment.

"I don't know. You better ask him."

"We surely will. And let me state one thing clear!" the captain raised his voice and in the silence that followed his words only the breaths and the humming of the transmitters were audible. "We are far away from home, from the Earth. We have covered just a half of our assumed distance. We cannot count on any help. But the laws here are the same as the laws on Earth, and I am here to make sure everyone follows them. And according to the law Rasmus is owned by Hornet, and she is the only one to decide whether or not let him pilot the ship."

Veronica shrugged.

"Is my decision of any importance? Have I got any real choice? I must accept. I won't let colonists die because I may fear for Brent and because I'd rather have him on my side."

"That thing cannot be harmed..." doctor Xiao murmured. "Don't you make a fool of yourself!"

"Cut it!" the captain shouted. "We are not here to quarrel! We have months of drudging through the Kuiper's Belt ahead of us! De Bernal, you are the chief navigator, what will you say to Rasmus piloting the broken *Viking*?"

Camus de Bernal looked confused. He had never assumed he would have to decide about such important matters. And he could foresee the consequences all too well.

"If we can keep in touch, then I see no contradictions. The droids are extremely precise, but they lack the instincts. If they cannot use logic, they fail. And that is why they must be supervised."

"That can be easily accomplished," said chief of computer technicians, Ivanov. "We can stabilize the connection between the bridges of *Viking 04* and *Viking 01*. Would that be sufficient?"

"That would do. The pilot on the bridge will be in a constant touch with Rasmus, who doesn't need the replacement."

"He does," Veronica interrupted. "Every two days he needs to re-charge, and it deactivates him for four hours."

"Not necessarily," O'Leary said. "He can charge through the steering console through the direct entrance panel. And that would be the best solution."

Two other droids were to remain in *Viking 04*. Roy 98D, engineer's Barbara Wong from *Viking 02* was trained as her assistant, so he could take charge of the ATs team and check the engine room. Rosamunde 305F, whose dominant was Brazankis, the pilot, was managing the passengers sustaining system well.

After the broken ship management was all set, the matter of colonel's Denberry broken spine needed immediate actions. A complex operation of inserting an implant that would conduct the impulses to the spine seemed impossible to be performed in space. And Veronica was able to construct the implant with the tools she had and the parts available on board, she just needed to use an electron microscope.

"I am not sure if we would succeed," Tengiz Gongadze said. "The success is a matter of microns, and the width of the implant tentacles covers only Angstroms. We will do what we can, though."

"The colonel agreed to be euthanized if we don't succeed," said Lisbeth Mall, the only qualified neurologist. "Let us all hope we won't have to perform that."

All the doctors hoped for that. They have already lost one man, who was so badly hurt that the only thing to do was to let him die with dignity. Since the Body Own Law was introduced, the doctors were forbidden to refuse anyone who wanted to finish his or her own life. That introduction didn't result in disrespectful treat of human life. On the contrary, it provided rapid growth of biotechnology, because the scientists would rather cancel all the disabilities with bio-prosthetics than assist to one another while killing people. Some new treatments of chronic diseases like diabetes and SM were developed and a suicide rate decreased. Knowing they could legally end their life any moment, most patients regained strength to fight the disease. And the doctors did what they could to help them.

Everyone knew that it would be not so easy in the colony, but at least they had knowledge and equipment to provide good medical assistance to the people. If they succeeded with a difficult operation in space, they would for sure manage on the ground. Gongadze had already made plans of a medical center, and when somebody told him it was well too early, he replied:

"The settlers used to build churches when they landed on new grounds. We will build a hospital. And believe me, it will be far more useful!"

His project was approved by the captain as one of the first facilities to be built on Patris.

XIII

We've been navigating through Kuiper's Belt for seven months. Viking 04 was partly fixed after the crush with the ice block. It is being navigated by android Rasmus 101A, who supervised constantly by the pilots of the mother ship.

The crew is exhausted, the morale going down. The Easyl and Opti supplies are low. Nobody wants to socialize anymore, the lectures and movie projections are no fun. We cannot wait to walk outside and step on a surface of a new planet. The women want to grow their hair long again, and we all crave to bathe, even in salty water.

Colonel Denberry is already cured and as fit as ever. Bio-implant made by Veronica Hornet was absorbed by his body with no complications. The remaining Viking 04 crew members assimilated well in their new roles. We didn't manage to recognize what caused the steering malfunction, we are only sure it wasn't another sabotage. It might have been some spontaneous spark that blocked the steering. It is all fixed now and we travel with no problems.

Ivo Hasek has been released from his prison cell and can move around the ship. He wears blue overalls to be recognized immediately and is electronically supervised. Keeping him locked was seen by all the crew members as cruelty.

David Sabatini is growing well. He has started to speak, but has some difficulties with learning to walk, but it is definitely caused by gravity changes. His psyche is stable, he isn't even conscious of his loss of the mother. Colonel Gongadze is first to adopt him once his wife is woken up when we arrive on the spot and the adoption procedures can be launched. Even though Gongadze and Oksana Wysocka were formally divorced, they decided to re-marry and form a whole family again.

"Miss Etta, what does "Irwin" mean?" asked Reina, and Etta raised her eyes from the chronicle entry she had been writing.

Reina wanted to borrow the second volume of *Human Behaviorism* from Raul. And since she wasn't here she decided to wait.

"Why are you asking me that?"

"Rivas wrote about "The Irvin's Law" in his book, but he didn't say where the name came from."

"It is not mentioned often, since nobody really cares. The law that allows The Nature Guards to kill any poacher at spot was named after a man who had fought for animals' rights, Steve Irvin. He lived in the days when people thought that attitude as somewhat weird. He died young, but he did a lot for animals."

"He wanted poachers to be killed?"

"No, Raina. He was a good man. He wouldn't hurt anyone. He showed that every animal deserves to be loved, even the species that cannot be hugged or kept at home. He made people realize that every life is sacred, and humans, as a species, shouldn't think they are privileged in any way."

Etta went silent; she felt confused. How could a phenomenon of naming a very restrictive law after a peace-loving man be explained to an android?

"Tell me, Reina, you don't really understand humans, do you?" the teacher asked.

"I don't, not at all. I know their patterns of behavior, but I don't understand the motives of them. I guess Rivas didn't understand them as well, he only described what he had seen. Miss Etta, can I ask you about one thing?"

"About anything."

"Why am I useless?"

"You what?"

"Every android has a function, I am the only one who just walks around master Kirk."

"That is your purpose. You are to guard the captain and be there if he needs you. If anything happens, you protect him."

"Why would I?"

Etta couldn't find any answer to that. The deer-like eyes were looking at her from a dark, smooth, emotionless face.

"Because… Because that's your nature."

Etta knew the answer was clumsy, and that the droid would probably not grasp the meaning, but she couldn't think of any better.

Raul, who has just peeked into the cabin, saved her.

"The captain asks your presence," he said. "Some important matter. A gathering."

"Again?"

Etta put her writing pod down and went out. Such unexpected meeting could only mean trouble, and everyone was sick with trouble. The morale and low mood among the crew was enough trouble. Jewel was close, but not close enough to say that the journey was done. Even though they knew there was nothing to be done in the matter, everyone nagged about monotone food and poor water ratios. Another troublesome issue could result in riot that would have to be quenched by force. And using force in space was always fatal.

O'Leary, silent and gloomy, joined Etta on her way. He looked bad: his face sunken, lips cracked, some nervous sparks in his eyes. There was definitely something wrong with him.

"What is wrong with you, Mac?" She stopped and forced him to do likewise.

"Nothing."

"Don't you nothing me here, I can clearly see you are not all right!"

"You got some water to share?"

Etta produced small flask, which she always carried with her, like soldiers. Sherman LaVer wanted his people to be ready for any disaster, and that would mean carrying water, nutrient pills, knives, torches and first aid kit with them wherever they went. The basic equipment meant twenty five percent higher chances of survival in case of emergency.

O'Leary grabbed the flask and swallowed greedily.

"Thank you," he sighed, handing her the bottle back, "You saved my life."

"What did you do with yours?" the girl scolded him, and he only shrugged.

"And what do you think? Moonshine isn't made of stolen algae and yeast, is it?"

"Are you out of your mind?"

"No. I just need a drink from time to time!"

"You risk dehydration to make booze and poison yourself? You waste your ratios for that?"

"I guess that's what I do!" he looked at Etta with irony and challenge. "Are you going to report it? I broke some rules, didn't I?"

She shook her head.

"You risk dying to get drunk! Why?"

"Because I like it, that's why, my dear. And our laboratory is a perfect distillery, since after the biologists' shift no one is there. I don't even need a battery to..."

"At least be cautious enough and don't get caught, will you? We are here, let's talk about that insanity later."

"Whenever you wish, princess!"

They entered the hall together, almost all the seats already taken. The video screens hanging on the multi-tentacle holder were showing the halls of the remaining ships. Only the *Viking 04* screen was dark.

"Is everyone here?" asked the Captain, but it wasn't really a question. "Turn all your attention to me now! Our pilots spotted a strange object. It is not an ice meteor nor a rock. Our research shows that it is a spaceship."

The room rustled, the excitement rising, when the 3D visualization hovered over the table. It was impossible to claim it was something natural, not made. It had a firm body, a tail and wings suggesting it could move both in vacuum and in atmosphere of a planet.

"How big is it?" asked Leonid Derkacz. His sunken face was full of disbelief and surprise.

"Approximately ninety feet long, forty five feet tall, sixty feet deep." Camus de Bernal recited.

"Tiny shell. How did it get here?"

"I could as well ask you."

"Is that an alien shaft?" asked Silberstein. Her voice was trembling with emotion. She was dreaming of meeting aliens and deeply believed the ancient truth that they must be there. Somewhere.

"We cannot say. It is old. No spark of energy detected, no coordinate movement. It is just drifting. And I think we should examine it."

"What if we get infected with some alien bacteria?" asked Xiao cautiously. "It is only an unnecessary risk!"

"On the contrary. It is our duty, a debt we must pay to humankind."

"I volunteer!" Haynemann, a physicist from *Viking 03* shouted.

Others declared likewise, the heat of breaking the routine of a long, boring journey increasing.

"Order!" shouted the captain. "Nobody examines nothing now! If it is really an alien craft, it may be as well a deadly crap. I do not intend to lose any more men!"

"Don't be ridiculous, captain! Aliens?" Derkacz sneered. "We are the only aliens here!"

"So how did it get here? And who built it?" nagged Lisbeth Mell.

"Unless you give me an undeniable proof it was built by some alien civilization, I won't believe it!" Derkacz sealed his narrow lips.

"The only way to get that proof is to go there and examined it," noticed Woznansky. The possibility of putting his hands on an alien technology was making him dizzy and craving.

The captain was fighting inside, looking at his crew. The shaft had to be examined and he knew that. Not only to satisfy their curiosity, bit to open some new doors for humankind.

"I think we must."

He was interrupted by the appearance of a co-pilot who came into the room holding a data filer in his hand.

"We may have some answers, sir!" he said. "There are some signs on the side of the raft, we tried to sharpen the picture."

Willner put a crystal disc to a data reader and a dim picture simmered on the screen. Those were ordinary letters, forming a name of the ship: *ESS Stephen Hawking.*

The mutual sigh of disappointment rolled over the crowd.

Only O'Leary rubbed his forehead as if trying to remember something.

"*Hawking* crew went silent after the passed Jupiter," he said finally. "Is it possible that they got here?"

"That cannot be H*awking*!" Derkacz protested. "It is way too small. It must be a rescue shuttle. And now it is an obligation to go there and find something that would explain their sudden Missing. They had families, friends, who deserve to know!"

"But it was too long ago," Kaori said from the screen. "Nobody awaits that news now. As far as I remember *Hawking* was launched over fifty years ago. Two years later the Global Space Program was cancelled, giving no results and generating absurd costs. The only remnants of it are two space stations still probing the moons of gas planets and the Venus observatory *Max Planck.*

Veronica gave the captain a pleading look, so he pointed to her.

"The program was canceled only officially, just to sooth public opinion. The research continued. If they weren't, it wouldn't be possible to send the ships to Patris and establishing *Michio*. The *Vikings* would have been impossible to build if the scientists of *Global* and *Explore and Migrate* programs didn't work together."

O'Leary burst with laughter.

"I always claimed that the government was a bunch of liars!"

"Silence! I won't have any politics here!" Willner silenced him. "Stanislas Novak from *Viking 05*, you are responsible from now on to drag the wreck closer to the convoy."

"Yes, sir!" the broad face of a middle-aged man with a "perfect balanced" tattoo on his temple appeared on the screen.

"Take a shuttle and get the shipwreck here. Be careful and keep online with the mother ship!"

"Yes, sir!" Novak was beaming with pride, excited to be the first to see this time capsule that was the wreck.

"Why do they have those tattoos?" whispered Etta to Veronica.

"For emergency reasons. Both "perfect balanced" and "genetically useful" are the most valuable units in our society. In case of emergency they must be taken care of first. And they are the first to command."

"And Willner isn't?" So why is he the captain, and not, let's say, de Bernal?"

"Oh, but he is! He only chose not to get the tattoo. Having it is not required by law, it's kind of a badge of honor, something to brag about. Some would give a lot to have it."

The talk was over, because the captain ordered everyone to go back to their work.

The shuttle had to be examined carefully. It definitely was one of the rafts of *ESS Stephen Hawking*, and it was preserved almost intact, with only small scratches on its outer shell. After filming it from every angle the examination of the interior began. There were just a few people in the crew: Callum the biologist, Heynemann the physicist, doctor Linde, engineer Bahrani and two security guards. They all stepped inside through the sleeve. They were wearing overall suits and oxygen masks. Linde and Callum demanded an extra decontamination compartment between the shuttle and the *Viking*. The engineers were not happy with the extra work, but no one knew what they would find inside.

The shells of the shuttle were intact, so there was no decompression, the oxygen level was around ten percent, the air inside wasn't breathable. The atomic reactor was also whole and intact. Bahrani judged that it died after the uranium fuel was all burned down, and the cooling system worked all the time. The pipes were wringed and empty now, the cooling liquid evaporated, leaving the whitish residue in the cracks.

The shriveled mummy of a pilot was still in his seat, wearing rugs that used to be a navy blue uniform. The sleeves with gold straps and a shiny emblem on the left lapel were still there, but the material on the chest was as if rotten.

"It looks like something has eaten him from the inside..." Aisha Bahrani nervously turned her head.

"We'll see," Kenneth Linde answered, "The body must be transported to the lab for an autopsy. Give me a thermo-insulating cover, those ice mummies would fall apart in higher temperature.

"I want to assist at the examination in the cool room." Callum declared. "I will take some samples for my team."

Bahrani's face turned pale. "I hope we won't bring any alien creature to the ship," she whispered under the clear cover.

"Stop this fantasizing, will you?" he biologist murmured. "It is probably the effect of natural decomposition. The inner bacteria from the guts start to eat their host, producing gases, the body swells until the gas release, and then collapses, so the soft tissues-"

He stopped, because Bahrani's face turned green. She lifted her hand pointlessly and Callum was afraid that she would just puke on the plastic.

"Calm own and breath deep," he instructed her. "Don't you dare to vomit, you will choke to death!"

Bahrani didn't want to die like that, but even though she managed to gather her bearings, Cynthia Heynemann had to take her spot. The engineer went back to her ship and didn't eat for the next two days.

It took a week to make a report.

"The pilot died of lack of oxygen and hypothermia. The body decomposed partially, than was mummified. There were no papers in the pockets, so we don't know the pilot's name. Two of his ribs got broken shortly before his death, there were no other injuries. He wasn't sick, nor underweight. He was around thirty, I assume."

"The malfunction of heating and air conditioning system was the direct cause. The pilot died, but the machinery started to run again, and continued for two weeks or so," Olenska, the technician from *Viking 02* added.

"It would explain the partial decomposition," Gongadze continued. "We found no toxic substances in the tissues, and the fact that the body was still seated in the pilot's spot suggests that he wasn't even aware of the malfunction. He just lost consciousness."

"The shuttle's auto diagnostics is dead," Olenska again, "so he was likely to just fall asleep and collapse."

"At least we know he didn't suffer." the captain said gravely. "Something to add, Callum?"

"Nothing of higher importance. There are some microscopic life forms in the samples, not classified on earth, so they probably come from Patris. They breathe oxygen, so it would confirm our assumptions considering the planet's atmosphere. The food and water supplies were used in a quarter part. They were typical military ratios. We didn't find anything else."

"Olenska, you were running the steering control. What can you say about it?"

"Apart from the auto diagnostics all other systems seem to be still working. Apart from the black box we have found some data holder that was connected to the transmitter. Pavlov/s team is struggling to read it."

"Why are they struggling?"

"The holder is ancient, and it was beaten by some magnetic whirlwinds... Part of the data is gone and the holder won't fit any of our reading devices. Woznansky and Silberstain are trying to build one using the components of the shuttle's steering console. We are not sure if the data can be read at all."

"What about the black box, Pavlov?"

The chief of I.T. technicians raised his head.

"We only managed to read the planned shuttle's course so far. The pilot was to take it out of Schoumaker's Belt to the point from which it could send a message towards the Earth. That would explain the situation. *Michio 1* was shut down then, *Michio 2* was not built yet, because the robots constructing it were in no rush. The only way to send a signal to earth was to send a shuttle beyond the belt. And that was the poor man's assignment."

"He gave his life for nothing..." commander Halama sighed.

"Are you sure he didn't manage to send a signal?" asked Etta.

She couldn't sand the idea of this brave man dying in vain. The nameless hero must have known that he had minimal chances to succeed, alone in the tiny shuttle. He must have tried to send the signal. He didn't foresee his sudden, painless death, even before he managed to use half of his supplies. He was aware that he would drift in cold, empty space for weeks. And he decided to do it. All in vain.

"No signal reached the earth, *Hawking* was declared gone with no trace. The pilot must have died before he managed to get out of the discus. The engine pushed him forward for some time, and it took it fifty years to drift to this point."

"We must read the data, we owe him that," said Sasha Krasusky.

After the *Viking 04* crash Krasusky was nominated by Willner to be his deputy, as the most suitable officer.

"What had happened with the rest of the astronauts?" Yoko Kaori asked.

"We will know once we decipher the data."

"I cannot understand one thing," Callum was wondering. "How come we came across the wreck? It is like a speck of dust in this huge belt area! The probability of finding it was minimal!"

All turned their attention to Nova, the only pilot present.

"It is not as impossible as you all assume. Kuiper's Belt is a complex structure. It has less dense spaces, like currents, similar to Cassini's crest in Saturn's ring. One of it is the shortest course from Earth to Jewel, and it runs through Schoumaker's Discus. It is the obvious course of *Hawking,* so they sent a shuttle through it."

„We were lucky to come across it." O'Leary cut the discussion. „It would be easier for two mosquitos to meet in the jungle if they started from two different edges of the continent."

„Let's not waste our time to think about our luck." said the captain in a dry voice. „The medics will secure the pilot's remnants, we will bury him once we get to Patris. And I.T. team, you continue on the data gathered from the ferry."

„And what about the shaft itself?" asked Camarro.

„We leave it behind. It is not a toy, you cannot just put it in your pocket."

„I wish I could," Camarro murmured with disappointment. She wanted to roam about a wreck, but she couldn't object the captain's order.

***

Stiepan Pavlov and his team managed to gather the data from the black box and the device they found in the cockpit. Woznansly and Silberstein managed to construct the data reader so they all could now drudge through deciphering and clearing the data. It was essential to read everything they could, as there were not only information about the malfunction and S.O.S. signal there, but the whole history of the journey. The document would provide valuable information both for the crew and for the Earth archives. The technicians worked twenty four seven before entering the Schoumaker Discus would unable communication.

„I wish Brent was here to help us," Veronica dreamed while walking back from the gym with her friend. „I Miss him a lot, you know."

„I can imagine that. But at least you have Sherman. It is nice to hug such a big bear, isn't it?" Etta liked to tease her buddy when they were both in good mood. She knew all too well that the bear-like major was no teddy bear at all.

„It is! He is the greatest man I have ever met!"

„He claims you deserve better."

„Bull-shit! His self-esteem is way too low! He would fit perfectly in my..." Veronica bit her tongue. „It is good to know that Brent is managing so well."

„Where would he fit so well, hmm? Finish the sentence."

Veronica just waved her hand.

„Well, he would fit into my genotype. You know, breeding. The government weights the idea of allowing some of the highest quality zeros to breed. They have worked on some method of fixing bad genes. We would become ones, or even twos after such fixing. We need more babies, that's for sure."

Etta looked at her friend. Who would suspect that such a perfect body harbored also a perfect mind? Even with her head shaved Veronica looked more like Egyptian princess and not like a lice infected ramshackle, as O'Leary used to describe the women on board. He thought it funny, but they thought otherwise. Most of them really looked bad with no hair, only Veronica and Commander Marjem Halama looked alluring with bald heads.

"You know so much," Etta thought that Veronica knew even more, but was just secretive.

"I actually do. I used to work for secret service, remember? But please, don't ask me. I tell only what I can tell."

"They wouldn't chase you here for spilling government secrets here, don't you think?"

Veronica laughed.

"You are so sweet and naive, Etta!"

Etta didn't know how to understand that. Her gaze was questioning, so Veronica dragged her out to provide some explanations.

"Have you ever noticed the conclusions we are drawing out of this journey about humanity?"

"That the humanity is strong?"

"Well, no. That is not the point. The point was to migrate before humans, crushed with boots of totalitarian system, and pampered by technology, would lose all its vital qualities. Do you get it?"

"Actually, I don't."

"Just think about the course of the latest history. We've been euthanizing malformed babies and fatally ill for centuries. We neutralize killers and mentally conditioned, those, who cannot be cured. But we here, the crew, we were fighting like lions for a life of one baby, even though it was endangered with being crippled. We would spare us all so much trouble if we but put David to sleep. It was legal. And we didn't kill the saboteurs who could have killed us all, instead we've just found a way to send them away. Isn't that enough for you? The crew had showed mercy for Hasek, who impersonated the security guard member and tried to destroy the mother ship. And we all wanted to run to save the crew of *Viking 04*. Do you understand the meaning of all that?"

„I think I have just started to understand..."

„Exactly. There is still hope for us!"

XIV

Etta woke up with a feeling that something terrible was going on.

She was lying still, chasing the last clear memory of the previous evening, but her stream of consciousness was as if cut with a sharp knife. Her body was heavy as if made of led, she could barely breath. She felt hands on her face, but could not open her eyes, the light that hit them through the cracks in her lids was blinding. Her body was aching, as if she had been badly beaten up, every breath was a struggle, as if an iron clamp was being put around her chest. And if that wasn't enough, somebody tried to put something into her mouth.

Etta narrowed her eyes and recognized Raina's tawny face. The droid was trying to force open her jaw and slide a cold metal object inside, right between her teeth. Was she trying to kill her?? Why would she do that?

Etta panicked, trying to push Raina's hands away, but her body wouldn't co-operate. Was her spine broken?

„Let me go," she murmured. „Leave me, what you doing?"

„Open your mouth, Miss."

Etta felt the steel once more, tasted metal on her tongue. She twisted her head.

„Let me be! I did anything wrong! Don't kill me, please! The captain and me, we aren't… Raina, don't do this!"

The droid let her go and Etta heard her calling:

„Raul come here at once!"

Raul's face appeared in front of Etta. He placed his hands on her shoulders and shushed her, as if she were a baby.

„It is going to be all right. Don't you worry. You have to open your mouth now and let us put the tube in your throat, you won't be able to breath in this gravity."

What gravity?"

„We've reached almost four G now. Listen to me, Etta, I need to give you some cryostatin."

„No! Don't put me to sleep, please!"

Etta cried with fear and helplessness, even though she could barely breathe. Cryostatin was being used to put people into a drug-induced coma, it lowered body temperature and slowed the metabolism down. It could also cause some shock after the patient was being brought back.

Raul wiped Etta's tears away, all patient and calm:

„I need to do this, otherwise you won't manage through the Schoumaker's. It will take a week to fly through it."

„But… what happened?"

„The gravitation systems broke. Etta, trust me. You've always trusted me. I would never mean you any harm."

Etta was lying helpless, her heart racing, her chest barely moving.

„I trust you. Do what you must."

Raul let her go and she felt a pressure of a needless syringe on her bared arm. She had never been put to sleep before, but after a few seconds her fear was gone, melted away in numbness. She only managed to wonder: Would she ever be woken up again?

„Is she already asleep?" asked Raina.

„She is. Turn the oxygen on." He lowered the syringe and put a monitoring band round his Domina's arm. The miniature screen flashed, ready to show her heart rate. Raina had finally managed to intubate the woman. She put a drip up and went away to double-check the remaining members of the crew, who laid dormant side by side.

„I'm going to the deck now. Roy is in the engine room, you take care of the humans. You check them every quarter and put the numbers down. Then you go to the passengers rooms. If all the lights are green, you come back here. If not, you inform the AIs. The scale of norm is on every screen in the middle. Just inform me if any of them isn't balanced. If something really bad happens, the monitor will tell you what to do. When the drip is down below the marked level, you put another on. You can go to reload to the engine room in thirty nine hours. It should take you the quarter you got free between the rounds."

„Copy that. I follow your instructions. „Raina looked at Etta. „Why did your dominatrix think that I tried to break her?"

„To kill her," Raul corrected her. „I don't know why. Humans just can't control their software. And then they think wrong. It is of no importance now."

He was talking as calm as he was acting. If he were a human he would act in anxiety and stress now, but luckily he wasn't. Having no emotions whatsoever was a blessing in their present situation.

The gravitation systems started to malfunction right after *Vikings* entered Schoumaker's Discus. The sudden gravitation thug made most of people faint, some of them unable to move, or even think clearly. The blood rushing off their brains made them unable to understand what had actually happened. Only doctor

Xiao managed to stay alert, as she was ready to inspect the passengers' cabins and she had her suit on. She panicked, seeing all around her drop as id dead. She wasted precious minutes to calm down and check on her lab screen the communicated from the main computer. After she had realized what happened, she started to panic even more. It took her three more precious minutes to realize she was probably the only conscious person on *Viking 01,* or even in the whole fleet.

„I won't give up!" she murmured, feeling the urine drip down her leg, but there was no one around to be ashamed of for wetting her pants in panic. She couldn't take the suit off, she had no time to lose, even though she didn't really believe she could do anything at all.

She was nauseated while drudging through the corridors, being afraid they were heading towards their end. She managed to the bridge and noticed that Joao Jimenez, the main pilot managed to put the shaft to autopilot before he collapsed. She also noticed through the vision holes that the remaining ships were formed, so all of the pilots must have done the same, or the only one that broke was *Viking 01.*

The doctor knew she was all alone in this. She put her oxygen to minimum, gaining half an hour or so, than she used her passwords to shut the security systems down. She found Raul bend over his Dominatrix and started to instruct him.

„We are going to continue like this and there is nothing to be done about that. The humans need medical assistance and there is no one here who would manage to do it. Will you and the droids be able to follow my instructions?"

Raul got up.

„Carry on, doctor."

„What can we do to contact other ships?"

„Light signals, Morse code."

„Can you use it?"

„No, but it is all in the book."

„Go fetch it, and bring Raina here."

They were back in no time.

„Now you listen to me. Even though I cannot believe you would manage to do it, it would be arrogant if I hadn't tried to use you. The thing to be done is..."

She instructed the droids what to do and how to pass the knowledge to the droids on the remaining ships. Before she collapsed, she managed to give them all the passwords and the codes of medical library and labs.

The droids worked in accord. They managed to use the Morse code efficiently. All the ships were the same, so the malfunction was a result of entering the discus. All the humans were put under oxygen mask, in emergency rooms, with cryostatin cruising in their bodies. The drips were put up, the muscles nurtured with medicine that would help them tense. One android on each ship piloted the ship to avoid meteors, and the autopilots kept them on course. The meteors couldn't have been dodged though, so the lasers to crush them were ready and warmed up. The droids were perfect marksmen with their hands that have never shaken.

ATs took care of the engines. Raul managed to instruct the droids on all of the fleet ships. The passwords provided by the doctor made the whole operation swift, and Xiao wasn't to realize it for a while. After they crossed the discus, they just had to hit the brakes and wake the crew up. The droids were just following the orders, and they didn't hesitate for the next seven days. They didn't feel the drudge of time, they weren't fatigued, bored or anxious.

The crew was just about to know that they saved their lives after being woken up.

When Kirk Willner came around, he couldn't realize where he was for a while. The memories were uneager to co-operate. His body was itching as hell, and his physiology turned suddenly on him. Humiliated and disoriented, he tried to stand up, but only managed to sit. His sight went dark and he thudded again, hitting his head on the ground. The pain made him conscious again he cursed faintly. Some tawny, slender hands pinned him to the floor.

„Stay put, sir!" Raina's voice penetrated. „Cryostatin is not washed out of your body yet, your muscles must learn to react properly again. We are out of discus now, so the gravity systems are back to normal, but you were crushed by gravity for a week."

„I need to wash," the captain murmured, not really recognizing his voice.

„That is not prior now..."

„Hell you know what prior is!"

„Captain, you must wait a while, and then try to stand up slowly. Your blood pressure is still below the norm," Raina explained patiently, massaging his calves at the same time. „Take deep, even breaths and try not to think."

„Not to think? What the hell had happened here?"

Raina monologue and the explanation Raul had provided to her earlier, moving up to massage her Dominant's arms. Her voice cleared his mind, he could now remember the sudden pressure and the blur of people collapsing. Then all went blank, up to now.

„How are the others doing?" His voice was back to normal, not an alien, stubborn creature in his mouth anymore.

„One deceased. All others stable, waiting to be brought around. All hibernation capsules working properly."

„Who's dead?" asked Willner, pretending to be calm.

„Doctor Celine Xiao." Raina's eyes went blank, then she recited like a machine: „Cortisol level critically low. Electrolytes low, level up. Potassium dose. Blood oxygenation critically low. Ventricular fibrillation. Death hazard. Adrenaline shot, apply. Lidocaine dose, apply. Potassium dose, apply. Cardioversion. Defibrillation. Larynx swell. Adrenaline, apply. Atropine, apply. Tracheotomy now. Systolic critical. Brain swell. Time of death eight fifty four p.m."

„So it went..." Willner whispered.

„Raul didn't know what the medicine were. Before he manager to localize them, the heart stopped. We didn't know what tracheotomy was. The definition from the computer wasn't enough for us to perform it. We tried resuscitation, as we have known it from the first aid routine, but it was good for nothing. Are we to blame that Xiao ceased to function?"

Willner was silent, focused on rubbing hands.

„No, you are not to blame," he said finally. „I am sure you did everything right. None of you is a medical droid, and even MD wouldn't stand for a doctor. Am I ready to get up now?"

„You are."

Willner was all too eager to move from the stinking, sticky floor he was lying on. The members of the crew were there, all askew, not woken up yet. The monitors were pulsing attached to their arms, the air was filled with the hum of air being pushed into their lungs. As the gravity normalized, the oxygen pressure lowered and was now marked as optimal.

Raul stood in the door, waiting for the captain's orders.

„Wake them up. I'm going to the bridge. Just let me… change first."

„I have spare clothes ready for every member. I have also warmed the sterilization tubes and dry cleaning. The doubled water ratios, glucose cubes and protein pills are waiting for them in their quarters."

„I would give you a medal if you weren't the droid. Just wake them up and have the ATs clean this cesspool. When I'm back I want to see my face in the polished floor and smell roses in the air!"

Willner walked out, took a deep breath and headed to his cabin. He was so weak that he barely reached it. He gulped on water, put a glucose pill under his tongue and just then took the soiled uniform off. He felt more energetic, put a mask and switched the cleaning tube to maximum level for ten minutes.

I would give my kidney for a hot shower, he thought, feeling the ozone gushes lashing his body. *Or a bathtub full of scented bubbles…*

It was all but a wishful thinking. None of young cadets thought of those unpleasant aspects of space travels. None of the lecturers were eager to talk about that, just to keep cadets enthusiastic.

Water or no, the tube worked well and he felt sparkling clean, his body tingling like after a good rough rub. He put fresh clothes on, placed the soiled ones to a laundry collector. After drinking the rest of the water and swallowing two more pills he was ready to go back to the bridge and be the pristine, immaculate captain again.

The lights of the consoles were pulsing evenly, indicating the proper work of all the systems. Willner sat in his chair and called the remaining decks. He wasn't even sure they would answer; three of them had just one droid aboard and a small crew of ATs. Have they even understood the instructions provided them by old fashioned Morse code? But Rhonda 12F, Roger 7E and Ruslana 39F all reported the same: all of the crew members had been injected with antidote, they were just waking up, and no major problems were reported. Even Brent from *Viking 04* cut in to report that everything was all right.

They would never believe that back on Earth... the captain thought. *Even poor deceased Celine wouldn't accept the fact of how capable the droids were.*

Celine was dead, and the autopsy had to be performed. They would do that after the crew members regained their vital strength. Her death was too important to be ignored and the cause of it had to be known.

It took three days for all the crew members to be back on their feet. Everyone was back to their jobs, the systems all diagnosed and working well, so now they could Focus on Xiao and her actions.

„It is obvious," Willner stated after switching the transmission of her actions off, „that doctor Xiao had saved us all. She kept her bearings and instructed the androids what to do, so they could take care of us while we laid dormant. Even little Sabatini survived, and his survival is the peak of A.I.'s success. I have already noted down in the report the obvious point about praising doctor Xiao with post-mortem Honor League medal for her courage."

„I have some other point to ask about," said Derkacz. „Our gravity systems failed in Schoumaker Discus, but *Hawking* hadn't seemed to have such problems. Why?"

„Fifty years ago the technology of autonomic magnetic pulse systems weren't developed yet," Shamir Om, the engineer, explained. „The artificial gravity was created by analog rotation of rings. It was unbreakable."

„Its evolution, baby!" O'Leary sneered.

He was thinking about Xiao's corpse, lying motionless in the fridge somewhere in the bowels of the ship. He couldn't believe that the woman, so full of life and determined, just gave up. He couldn't care less about the tech details of *ESS Stephen Hawking*. Now, when the bitter and sarcastic doctor was gone, he realized how much he had cared about her. The sorrow inside of him was like fossil sucking the will of life out of him.

He stood up and headed for the exit, ignoring the questioning looks.

Etta excused them both and rushed after her friend, and when she caught him she clasped his hand comfortingly.

„I know," she whispered. „We are all mourning. She was brave, and worthy."

The Irishman gave her his most ironic look.

„What does it matter now? Worthy or unworthy, we are all just a piece of cold meat in the end. Well, unless someone believes in some afterlife crap."

„And you don't?"

„Do I? I don't know. I descend from the believers. My mother used to tell me about the Great Timeless, but you know how it is nowadays. Not many are eager to claim that they believe anything apart from Fermat theory and Heisenberg rule."

„Well…" Etta hesitated. „I am privileged, I guess. We, historians, used to study the old world religions. I read a couple of versions of *The Bible, The Koran, The Mahabharata,* some Buddhist treaties, the Egyptian *Book of the Dead,* all of the mythologies… I wrote a paper on all those in my fourth year. The old cults were really beautiful. I wish they weren't gone."

O'Leary just nodded with his longish face, even longer in his sorrow.

„The concepts behind religions were beautiful, but you know better than the rest what came out of them. Some irrevocable crimes were made by people who shouted gods' names. That is why after the eco collapse all cults were banned and the shrines were turned into museums. It had to be done, but we both know how long people rebelled against the new law."

"I just can't understand why people had fought so fiercely for their beliefs, more than for food or water. We all can believe what we choose, there is no need to inform everyone around about our choice. Or even more to fight for it. The belief is in the mind."

O'Leary touched Etta's shaved head with the softness of caressing a child.

"That is human nature, kiddo. You can read all about the religion, but you'll never understand it, because you are a child of the modern era. All we can do is look up in the stars and think that there is something out there. Something which is the beginning and the end of all of it. It there is a force like that, for sure it resides in the realm we cannot reach. And for sure we cannot communicate."

"But why wouldn't we? I read a treaty of Vincent Parker once, but I cannot agree with him. It The Great Timeless really exists, why is he silent? Why wouldn't we be able to understand him? Our brains are the most perfect brains in the whole galaxy! We can reach the stars!"

O'Leary produced his flask and sipped from it. The intensive aroma of the alcohol made Etta's face twist slightly, but she didn't say a word.

"My child, it is all the matter of scale. Drosophila flies have thrived through millions of years. Try to explain to a fly what the seasons are, if it only knows one summer day in which it is hatched, breeds and dies. In the old days the earth was populated with huge apes. They were intelligent enough to understand the sign language, you know, that hand speech that had been used by un-euthanized cripples. They weren't neutralized in the old days, so they had to communicate somehow. So," O' Leary sipped some more. "Imagine that you own an ape like that, the one that can show you that it is hungry and it likes you. And now try to explain higher mathematics to a creature like that. That is the scale. So, it The Great Timeless really exist, even if he's been talking to us for eons, we wouldn't understand. We wouldn't even be aware that somebody is talking to us. So why would he bother?"

"And the afterlife?"

"The main problem with the afterlife is that one day we all come to know the answer. We just cannot word it back to the living. I'd rather remain rational. If in the moment of my death my consciousness soars towards heavens, it would be a pleasant surprise. Well, we'd see if it were pleasant or not. Generations of religious leaders were unable to prove that it really happens. But the other side of the coin is that none of the scientists ever managed to prove that such thing doesn't happen."

Etta felt that the bitter scientist struggled to believe his mother's word in the very moment.

The Chinese doctor and him, they developed some deep bond in the last few months, but of course he wouldn't admit it to anyone.

"I am so very sorry," Etta whispered. "I know that doctor Xiao was someone special. You shared some ideas, well, apart from your love for the droids."

"That's ironic, isn't it? The person who was uneager to state that the androids have human intelligence, had to trust them in a crucial matter. We will never know what her thoughts in that critical situation were."

He looked to the floor. They shared a moment of silence that was interrupted by Reina.

"The Captain asks all of the crew to come to the bridge." she just commanded with a dull voice.

"To the bridge? What the hell for?" O'Leary asked.

Reina twisted her head, her voice changed to a sweet tweeting.

"I asked him the same question, and Kirk answered: "Just get them all here, Raina.""

The doctor smiled with just the corners of his lips. This one never answered with some predictable scheme. She adorned her answers with individual remarks. And those voice chance, as if she tried to be flirtatious. All of that marked her uncommon, and O'Leary loved uncommon droids.

"Let's go, then," he said. "One has to obey the commander!"

All of the human crew gathered and crowded in the small space of the bridge, looking with heavily beating hearts and the control schemes that flashed in front of them.

Camus de Bernal voice rustled from the main speaker:

"We are switching to visual mode!"

The screen went black and then, in the space in front of the ship's nose, the specks of distant stars appeared, and there, among them, sparkled the round pearl of a planet.

"Jewel..." Sherman LaVer whispered. "Now I know why they named her like that!"

"It is beautiful!" engineer Silberstein chirped.

The captain chuckled to hide his emotions and said:

"That is out new home. We won't reach it in a day or two. It may take up to two months till we reach Patris. But from now on, everyone who would feel the pressure of the long trip, will be able to come here and look at our new sun, getting bigger and bigger with each passing day."

He looked at Ivo Hasek, who stood motionless, with his gaze glued to the screen."

"We are almost there, as you can clearly see." the captain said.

"I can see. It is really pretty. But it is not the sun. And the planet you are taking us to is not Earth."

XV

Our journey is finally approaching a closure.

The pilots diagnosed and stabilized the connection with the automatic space station Michio 2. The data from the last week has been collected from its memory bank. Every crew member was provided with the information of our families, our dear ones we have left behind. We really needed that. The new orders are also known to us all.

Right after we land on the surface of Patris we are to report the atmosphere and topography conditions, and we are to continue to report all of our actions. All we know for now is that the planet is pretty wild but suitable for human species. We cannot see it with our own eyes just yet.

Xiao's autopsy revealed that both of her adrenals broke and a large thrombus blocked the left chamber of her heart. Tengiz Gongadze has never seen anything like that. Whatever action the androids would take, they wouldn't have been able to save her. It is doubtful that the qualified medic team could prevent her death.

The crew members have already recovered after being applied large doses of multi-vaccine. Two soldiers from Viking 02 and an engineer from Viking 05 had an episode of seizure. There were four cases of diarrhea and twenty seven cases of fever that attacked lymph glands (noted from the medical report of Tengis Gongadze, the main physician). The vaccination is supposed to mobilize our bodies to meet all the unknown threats and microbes of Patris. The biologists claim that we would be able to produce antidotes in an hour to every possible bacteria or viruses we are very likely to approach. The multi-vaccine is the latest biomedical creation, but it has many unpleasant side effects that we cannot eliminate yet. The crucial thing is that we all survived it and the blood test show we have developed immunity.

We are still working on deciphering the message that was to be sent to the Earth by ESS Stephen Hawking. The chief I.T. engineer Pavlov won't stop working on that, by now he had only managed to read a few words and the final sentence that says "It is a bad planet." Is it a despair statement? Or a warning?

The crew members feel better since they can see Jewel, and even more enthusiastic since Patris appeared. Everyone follows procedures, no one needs to be disciplined. The captain released all the prisoners from their home-confinement. Corporal Hansen for being late for his service and doctor O'Leary who had been caught drunk. Only Ivo Hasek remained in confinement which resulted in his suicidal attempt. He remains in a drug-induced coma. Once the colony is established the doctors plan to run some psychotherapy.

We cease to shave our heads; we watch movies and dance once again.

Etta put the writing device down and her thoughts drifted to the previous night. Veronica threw an old-fashioned dance party that night. Elsa Silberstein unscrewed all of the chairs and tables in the canteen, then decorated the room and put some colored filters upon the lights. The masks were made by one of the nurses, Irina Kral, and corporeal Svensen provided some music that used to be fashionable when they were leaving the Earth.

The crew of the mother ship had times of their lives, like if it were some prom. Etta danced with the captain and with O'Leary. She almost forgot where they were. The thought of feeling the real ground under her feet was overwhelming. They were all oblivious to the difficulties they were about to face on the hostile planet.

And it was close, closer with every passing day. They could see it turning slowly, the perfect orb covered with brown, green and blue spots. It wasn't as blue as the Earth. There weren't any oceans or seas, even though it harbored plenty of water. The reports on the atmosphere and topography was being constantly analyzed by all qualified members of the crew. And the readings were promising. The air was likely breathable, with twenty three oxygen percentage, and that was even more than in the Earth atmosphere. The nitrogen level was slightly lower, and the remaining gases were an undefined but harmless mixture. Some carbon dioxide and methane indicated the photosynthesis and the presence of some creatures that breathed and digested.

Plants. Animals. Did it all mean that they could really live there, in the open, in the wild? Were the humans born and bred in the sterile conditions of closed cities really able to live there? Nobody but eco-certified citizens ever encountered any "nature". There were some birds in the cities, and huge butterflies with almost invisible, yellowish wings. Some said that there used to live millions of then, thousands of species of creatures shining like jewels. Nobody had really believed that and the ones that were froze forever in acrylic samples were thought to be fake. No one had ever seen those colors.

And the animals? They were just the exhibits in the museums. The only living creatures Etta had ever encountered were those that were about to be eaten: the selectively bred pigs that developed into the heaps of meat, bald and motionless rabbits. Only little chicks were slightly interesting: yellow and fluffy, chirping while dabbling at their food. The people visiting were not allowed to touch them, though, to minimize the risk of infection.

The richest people owned pet cats sometimes.

Etta had seen that gorgeous creature just once. When Major Montepietro's daughter asked her to come to her daughter's birthday party. Even though Etta's family was of lower social sphere, Major Alcantas cherished the idea that her daughter was befriended with well-behaved, doll-face girl marked with a stamp of being "a zero" in her early days. Some sad smile crawled on Etta's face when she thought about that party thrown in a splendid mansion. The orchestra was playing, the food and drinks were being prepared in the best restaurant and each of the little guests was presented with a little gift. But it was the cat that were the most beautiful: its slender body, graceful head and the coat of smoke-colored, shiny hair, it was lying on the pillow and looking at the guests with bright, golden eyes. When she was allowed to slide her hand along its back, a spark of envy towards Viola appeared.

Etta cried through the long night hours, embittered by the fact that her parents were too poor to afford such a gorgeous creature. Why had Viola have it all: that big house, sweets to eat and splendid dresses to wear, her summer trips to the real, not holographic, sea, and her beautiful cat? And she was numbered as "tree"! That was just unfair. It took Etta a couple of days to confess all that to her mother.

Etta's mother was a wise woman. She put her little daughter in her lap and explained:

"If you want one thing another person has, you have to know that you would have to take the whole package of another's life. You wouldn't like to trade with Viola. She is sick, and the best doctors cannot do anything to prevent her from dying in a year or so. Be glad that you are healthy, that you have strong body and witty mind. Not many of the kids your age have both.

It was the first time Etta realized that people can go and never come back again. That was how the cat made her childhood end, even though she hadn't realized that fact then. And Viola passed away a couple of months later, not realizing how close her friend was to hating her.

Raul lifted his gaze from reading.

"Why are you not writing?" he asked. "Is something wrong? Your face is wet."

Etta wiped her cheeks, embarrassed by the fact that she had let him see her weakness.

"It's just a memory. Irrelevant. What are you reading?"

"A biology treaty. I decided to learn to become an AM."

The girl opened her eyes widely, the air gone from her.

"What??"

The droid stood up, putting the reading device away.

"Don't be mad at me. I've been thinking about it a lot, for months, and now I know that this is what I desire."

"Isn't it enough for you that you are an AC?"

"I will still be an AC, but I crave to be something more. Try to understand me, you've always had. You used to say that I am not your property, neither your slave."

Cause you aren't. But I've never imagined that you could have your individual aspirations. Please, forgive me."

"So you won't stand against it?"

"Of course I won't! AM will be of a great value in the colony. But tell me one thing. Is that because I have failed you in some way?"

Raul just tilted his head questioningly.

"Maybe you think I do not need you anymore?"

"No, that's not it..." Raul paused, searching for the right words. He was never verbatim, even though his vocab increased systematically.

"I am not fully yours," he said finally. "I am party my own."

Was it even a coherent statement? He looked at Etta, as if panic-stricken.

"Is that bad?" he asked, unsure.

"Of course it is not bad. You are developing, so you are not satisfied with what you got anymore. You are looking for your own way."

Was it what a mother would feel when her child made a conscious decision for the very first time? She felt an unexpected stab in her heart, as if something has just changed irrevocably.

She paced towards her Companion to place her hand on his shoulder.

"Whatever you decide, I am here to support you." she promised.

The intercom rattled and spoiled the moment, and the captain's voice filled the air:

"Attention! We are approaching the orbit. The first scout team, prepare for scanning the ground. I do not need to remind you to put your suits on!"

No matter how safe Patris seemed to be, they all needed to be cautious. No matter how protective the multi-vaccine was, it was better to be cautious than die of some unknown germ. The first team was to collect the samples and come back to the mother ship. Only after decontamination and thorough examination were they to decide if it were safe to step on the new ground with no protective cover of the suit.

Even though they were all craving to feel the ground under their feet, they just watched the scouts ferries land in different parts of the globe and come back with the samples of soil, air and water.

"It is damned beautiful!" the scouts said, and all were listening greedily. "It's like the best video simulation ever! The sky is not so blue, well, it is kind of pinkish-bluish, and Jewel it seems to be bigger than our sun. And the plants, they are so juicy green, as if painted!"

All the test results proved the readings, that were being sent to earth for decades, correct. Patris harbored water, the same as one they had known on Earth, and soil that could be cultivated. The air was clean and even the microbes looked familiar.

"It is not so surprising." Callum explained. "The scientist of the twentieth century has already proven that the space contains just a bunch of elements, and no new ones had been discovered for centuries. I remember the euphoric reactions to discovering some simple sugars somewhere far away in the space. Well, the complex organisms that had developed in the galaxies far, far away may look like nothing we know, but they consist of the same materials as we do."

"Are the viruses, fungi and bacteria potentially harmful?" the captain asked.

"We cannot tell, they mutate too rapidly. Once we get sick, we can tell, but nothing looks harmful so far."

The decision on landing has been made, but it took them two more days to find the landing built by the robots and the outlines of the buildings that had already been prepared: sleeping containers, small power plant and water supply, all positioned at the foot of a beautiful mountain. Were they surprised that the robots managed to complete the project, and that it was so splendid?

"That is the end of our trip, our goal, our bull's eye!" The captain sounded enthusiastic. "Sasha Krasusky takes command here, while I land with the first crew, mostly scientists and guards. We'll scan the grounds and make sure it is safe for the rest to get out. The remaining engineers and pilots will take turns to stay on guard. We have fuel enough to cruise between the planet and the ships. The people who stay on duty on the ships take forty eight hours shifts."

All of the ships got into a heat, apart from *Viking 04* that has been piloted by androids. Those who were to land first were much envied. They didn't care, though, and they didn't intend to switch places with people who were to be left behind by now.

The captain returned to the bridge once more before boarding the ferry and instructed Jimenez:

"Send reports to the Earth, tell them that we are going down. The reply will be late, so I won't wait for it. You'll report it once we're back."

"Copy that."

Jimenes had serious difficulties with hiding his disappointment. Willner appreciated that he didn't protest, he could almost feel his anxiety.

"Don't worry, man. Everyone will be there in no time," he said comfortingly. "We are home. We just need to research it a bit before we wake the colonists up."

The captain was postponing the deed purposefully. He wanted to be sure that the conditions for living are stable, so he needed to get to know the new world. They wouldn't be harmed if they slept a little longer.

***

Four ferries landed in a rectangular formation on the plateau nearby a makeshift houses block. The captain, after confirming all the previous indications of the samplers, was the first one to jump down on the stony ground. He was surprised by the gust of wind. He has already forgotten how it felt. He has imagined the aromas of fresh greenery and moist earth, and he wasn't afraid to take the helmet off to smell them. He felt heavy, as if someone put a bag of bricks upon his shoulders and he realized, that the gravity here was a bit heavier than what they were used to aboard.

"Stay focused!" he commanded. "No jumping, no frolicking around! I don't want any fractures reported!"

"We are all likely to suffer from calcium deficiency," Gongadze raked his hand through his freshly grown hair. "I worry about the little boy. His bones have just started to develop, I hope he won't suffer any inconvenience here. The atmospheric pressure seems quite friendly at least. I'd rather not have dozens of sick people I'd have to stuff into one hyperbaric chamber!"

"I wouldn't be worried about that!" said Lebeth Mell. "But let us weight every step! We are all used to even surfaces and closed space. Let's stay together. Sorry, captain, for being so enthusiastic, but I speak as a doctor, cause the insubordination may cause only harm!"

Willner just waved his hand, cause his attention was focused upon the heard of creatures flying in a geometrical formation upon their heads. They were too big to be birds. Not many of those survived on earth. The air pollution caused the egg shells to be thinner with every passing year. Finally, when the air was barely breathable, the birds started to just fall from the skies.

Those here were some huge, heard animals, but they were too high up to be identified.

"Let's take a look at those shelters," Willner said once he realized that everyone was waiting for his commands. "It was properly built we will have a place to start. Follow me and no fooling around!"

The captain took a couple of steps and sprang back when the cloud of cigar-shaped insect, three pairs of wings each, puffed up like a cloud of smoke and disappeared in the thin air.

"It looks like we are going to have some fun here!" sneered Elrod Denberry, who was right behind the captain.

LaVer gave him a scolding look. They were all behaving like drunkards, engulfed with the air and all that wild life around them. Eyes were flashing in their pale faces, cheeks rouged from the wind.

"We surely will!" O'Leary murmured. "We know nothing about plants and animals living here."

He was the only one who didn't ooze enthusiasm. His raw, dry ironic way of looking at everything wasn't even scratched by the successful landing.

"We are here to learn!" Sakura, the chemist, answered. "We will examine each plant and each, even the tiniest, creature here!"

Willner stopped right at the edge of the plateau covered with something that looked like tall grass. He seemed confused, but there weren't eco laws here. One could step on anything, he assumed.

"Well, while we do not have any rules here, we can as well go through these plants. There is no other path anyway."

He started again, Reina one step behind, the others followed.

They moved in a line, trying not to damage to many plants. And they were a kind of grass indeed, but the blades were intricate, built more like feathers. Some unknown creatures were rushing through them, some feeding on them, all oblivious to the presence of another unknown creature: a human. Hordes of insects were filling the air, some silent, some buzzing fiercely. And humans were looking at them in awe. They only knew one species of butterflies, some flies and dragonflies that were rare to be spotted at the edges of water basins. Only eco-certified citizens were allowed to visit closed spaces harboring some more animals or insects.

And the colonists here felt like criminals, combing the tall grass, knowing that they were fracturing the delicate blades. Such behavior was unthinkable on Earth. The feeling was irrational and they knew it, but it didn't fade even when they reached the edge of the living facility. It was a bunch of tall, identical plastic blocks, seated at the foot of an ominous black mountain that reached the clouds.

"Well…" Woznansky was clearly disappointed. "They did what they could."

The robots didn't do a good job. Maybe the plans that were written into their software just hadn't worked in a different gravity conditions, or maybe something was shattered during the landing. The effect was that the buildings looked like misplaced Lego blocks. Only ten percent out of around three hundred cabins were solid enough to be inhabited. The rest had to be taken down, or re-built. The water pipes were clustered with mud and sand, shattered and crooked. Only the power plant that had been assembled on Earth looked pretty decent, but the wiring was pathetic.

The robots were standing in the far end of the facility, under a makeshift roof. Some of them beeped their standby mode once they indicated the presence of humans, but all of them needed renovation. O'Leary's and Derkacz's eyes sparkled once they put their hands on the machines.

Gongadze discovered a hall that was well insulated, so it meant it could be temporarily used as a medical center. So the engineers had their own place, and doctors alike. That way two teams wouldn't collide, but co-operate.

The women were interested with more practical aspects, so they went to examine the cabins. They were bigger than their spacecraft cells, equipped with the basic furniture like tables and beds. Each was a condo of a spacious room, small bathroom and a kitchen with electric cooking plate. Some place for storing the food and cupboards. It was promising. One just had to clean it thoroughly, put some linens on the beds and add some romantic curtains in the windows to feel like in a cozy twentieth century.

"If we work hard, we can live here in no time," reported Etta to the captain, she was making thorough notes for her chronicles. "The engineers say that there is no point in renovating the faulty cabins, because they are weather-beaten. And for us those which weren't are more than enough."

"What about the colonists?"

"Woznansky has an idea, but it will take him a month to complete his plan."

"So he'd better start now. I won't wake those people up unless I have their houses ready. And the power plant?"

"Shamir Om is working on it. The Uranium core is attached, the cooling system almost dome. Once he checks all the elements, he can run it. And for now we are to switch our batteries on, but it can be done after we finish to put the new wiring."

"How long?"

"Tomorrow. We will have power in all the cabins that are good enough to live in. There rest will be re-cycled."

Etta gave her pad to the captain for signing and sneezed.

"Did you catch some cold?" asked Willner while signing the report.

"Nope. It is from the air itself, the smell, and the pollen. I'm just not used to it. It is something completely new." She smiled shyly.

Sneezing was bad manners and she had been taught not to do it in front of anyone.

The captain patted her arm and walked away with Raina, always at his side, to check how the others were doing. He didn't say it loud, but he was extremely content of his crew's doings. They turned out to be quite reasonable and didn't lose their bearings on this seeming paradise. He was afraid that they would run around like crazy and breathe in the fresh air, but they just started to do their job. They were all disciplined, methodical, like if they were all soldiers. And the work was just flew, even though they were talking a lot and fantasizing about their great, future lives. So the captain noted down that the morale was super high and the good job was being done.

By the end of the day the whole facility was described and further works were scheduled. They voted as if they were one to take rooms here and stay for the night in the facility. The Jewel setting under the horizon and producing a spectacle that looked like aurora borealis made them stand gaping for a quarter, with tears in their eyes, speechless. Nobody was eager to go back to the ships after watching such a spectacle. They just opened their canned food ratios and ate it under the darkening sky. There were no moons, but two white spheres above, and those were Cesarea and Eppia, two remaining planets of the Jewel system. Cesarea was four times as big as the visible specks of distant stars, Eppia was six times big.

After they ate, they all went to their cabins, with the blankets they had taken from the ships, just in case. Just in case of sleeping on a foreign planet. And they all fell asleep immediately, tired and sheltered by the warm night. Only some soldiers remained on guard.

"Why would we need guards?" Silberstein asked. "There are no people around, just us."

"We are on alien grounds. We cannot imagine what can crawl out of the darkness," the commander answered. "We must be prepared for alien danger. That is why the guards stay awake, and I put movement detectors around the facility."

The captain was one of the guards, patrolling the grounds along with the soldiers, making notes and observations.

***

They were so overwhelmed with spending the whole day and night on a foreign planet that only in the morning, after taking a short nap, the captain thought about the report he had sent to the Earth. After thinking twice he decided that he would rather go back to the ship than calling them via the communicator.

Willner felt claustrophobic once he stepped back into the tight space of the craft. He couldn't say that aloud but he grew to hate it as a convict hated his prison cell. The thought about living her for months, for years, was repulsive. He went to the bridge while the shifts were changing.

Jimenez was sitting motionless, only his fingers were tapping at the edge of the countertop. The co-pilot was studying the monitors. Joao stood up when he saw the captain.

"Sit," Willner smiled. "What is the answer?"

"There is no answer, sir. There is only an incoherent buzz, on all the frequencies."

The captain's eyes widened.

"Did *Michio* brake?"

"No. We asked *Planck* for our saboteurs, and they answered that they were sent back to the Earth. So the transmitter works." Jimenez didn't have guts to admit that he was afraid to ask *Planck's* astronauts what had happened.

"Send the signal again!" commanded the captain.

"We do it every thirty minutes, sir. No effects, not even the usual control codes."

Kirk Willner was silent. What more was there to say? He had to remain calm, because he was responsible for those remnants of humanity, and he was about to organize their new life here. The blackest scenario was on, happening right now. And their new home was there, blue and green, specked with brown patches, so beautiful, and so alien at the same time.

"You are free to go. Take the next course to the surface," he said. "I stay here".

Jimenez just nodded, and they were out of the room.

The captain couldn't form a coherent thought for a while, he just tried to control his racing heart.

He sat in the first pilot's seat and gazed at the monitor.

The control signal was blinking, but the Earth remained silent.